UNHALLOWED MURDER
SIMON NASH

Also available in Perennial Library by Simon Nash:

Dead of a Counterplot
Death over Deep Water
Killed by Scandal

Unhallowed Murder

Simon Nash

PERENNIAL LIBRARY
Harper & Row, Publishers
New York, Cambridge, Philadelphia, San Francisco
London, Mexico City, São Paulo, Singapore, Sydney

A hardcover edition of this book was published in England by Geoffrey Bles Ltd. It is here reprinted by arrangement with the author.

First PERENNIAL LIBRARY edition published 1985.

Library of Congress Cataloging in Publication Data

Unhallowed murder.

"Perennial Library."
Reprint. Originally published: London : G. Bles, 1966.
    I. Title.
PR6005.H323U5   1985   823'.914   84-48614
ISBN 0-06-080758-X (pbk.)

85 86 87 88 89 10 9 8 7 6 5 4 3 2 1

UNHALLOWED MURDER

CHAPTER ONE

The two rows of cane-bottomed chairs creaked in disharmony like the members of a mutinous orchestra. The old clergyman sitting at bay behind the table facing them blew his nose and added a thunderous crescendo. As if in mockery of his catarrh, rain dripped down the windows and carried a stream of North London dirt to swell the flow of water and dead leaves into the churchyard next door. The parish room was cheerless enough to suggest a slight alleviation of the November night rather than a shelter from it. Modified cold and not real warmth came from the iron stove at the wrong end of the room, occasionally adding a puff of smoke to the stale air. The Church of England, scorned by her enemies as a prosperous bastion of the Establishment, offered to her friends only a thorough mortification of the flesh and a touch of holy poverty. In a mood suitable to the night, the Parochial Church Council was assembled.

A tall man with a quantity of curly grey hair was on his feet at the extreme right of the front row. With the deep, emphatic intonation of one accustomed to reading the lessons in a church with imperfect acoustics, he was reading aloud from a newspaper. It was a paper of small

7

but numerous pages and copious illustrations, a paper rejoicing in a large circulation though not one widely read by the clergy. This perhaps was why the Vicar was looking incredulous and sad over his handkerchief as the reading went on.

"We've been hearing about some pretty dirty work by a Church of England parson" – the tall man read – *"It seems that he's gone and served an eviction order on a poor mother who's trying to make a home for two children (and there's a third on the way) in a certain house in his parish.*

It's only a small house, and maybe the parson doesn't think it could mean much to anyone. But for this family it means Home. Now there's a young curate who wants somewhere to live. Fair enough. We don't expect a curate to sleep in the street. But the Vicar thinks that nothing but a whole house is good enough for another parson, even though he's a young, able-bodied bachelor. So the mother and her little children get notice to quit.

Somehow we don't think that this is the way to follow the Man who called himself the Good Samaritan. A man who wears his collar the wrong way round may have been a little dictator in the olden days, but we are not living in the Middle Ages any more.

Who does this Vicar think he is?"

The reading ended and the reader sat down. There was a concert of creaks as everyone shifted uncomfortably and the Vicar blew his nose in a muted, minor key. After a long silence, the tall man spoke again.

"Well, there it is," he said. "That shows the proportions this affair is taking. Now that the popular press has got hold of it, we shall be hounded day and night by reporters. I was never in favour of the idea, but as vicar's warden I felt it my duty to give it my support. Now, for the sake of the parish, I say that we must withdraw."

A red-faced man with a military moustache raised his hand in what appeared to be a political salute and looked hard at the Vicar.

"Yes, please, Mr. Farrow," the Vicar said feebly.

"I'm not speaking in my capacity as treasurer, but as a loyal member of this P.C.C. and therefore a servant of the parish. If I contradict my good friend Mr. Overley, I don't want him to take it amiss. He won't think there's anything personal when I say that his remarks are cowardly in the extreme."

Overley smiled urbanely and murmured that of course nothing could be less personal as an opening.

"My opinion is," Farrow went on, "that we mustn't let ourselves be intimidated. When you've brought your enemy out in the open, that's the time to face him and not run away. We learnt that on the Western Front, before some of the people in this room were born. Find his weakest point and hit it, hard and often. Now to begin with, this fellow hasn't been honest. He talks about a poor mother as if she were a widow or something. We all know that she's got a husband in a perfectly good job. Then he makes out that we're putting the Church before everyone else, but he doesn't choose to say that she's a niece of the Archdeacon of Wapping – who very sportingly hasn't tried to put his oar into the affair at all. The house belongs to the parish and we need it because our good curate is in digs half-way across London. So let's stand firm, with right on our side."

"The poor man is certainly uninformed," the Vicar said unhappily. "The idea that our Lord ever called himself the Good Samaritan is really most extraordinary. The epithet does not even appear in the parable, but is taken in popular usage from the page-heading that first appeared in —"

"Please, Vicar, may I speak?"

The man sitting next to Overley got up and broke desperately into the Vicar's words. He was a small, scholarly-looking man, plump and pink of face, with thin fair hair and rimless glasses. His name was Cyril Blanch, and he was people's warden. The Vicar sat back and disappeared behind his handkerchief again.

"The fact that we've got to face," Blanch said, "is that this house ought never to have been let for private occupation. As Farrow has said, it's a parish house and can rightly be used only for purposes directly serving the parish church. Its present use is improper and, in my opinion, illegal. By using it as a residence for one of the Parish clergy we are only restoring a situation that has become irregular. It isn't a question of who needs it most. We must let the eviction order stand."

Everyone looked at the Vicar, who blew his nose

again and appeared very downcast. His gentle eyes were red, perhaps from his cold and perhaps from something more. He cleared his throat twice before speaking.

"What you say is true, my dear Blanch, and I have to confess my guilt. I had no authority to allow the house to be used in this way, and I ought not to act on my own initiative in a matter of parish property and I really am very sorry. You know how much I depend on you all, my dear friends, to remind me about the regulations and so on, and I acted in a very impetuous and head-strong manner. At the time it seemed a simple act of charity for a family that had no home, when there was a house not in actual use – but there it is – I am so sorry –and I did arrange about this eviction order when the last meeting decided it —"

His voice trailed off and the members of the Council looked at the floor, for they were fond of the old man who served them devotedly and was continually getting the parish into trouble with some authority or other.

"Perhaps we ought to hear what the person most affected by the issue has to say." Farrow looked as he spoke at the young priest sitting beside the Vicar.

Everyone followed his glance, and the object of atten-tion blushed above his deep, new clerical collar. He was a well-built young man, not long ordained and carrying still an appearance of a student about to go out for a long training-run. His eyes had the blue innocence that already made him a favourite visitor to the devout old ladies of the parish, but there was firmness in his mouth and chin. When the Vicar smiled encouragingly, he spoke with diffidence yet with a manner that suggested an underlying confidence which the years would deepen into authority.

"This is all rather embarrassing for me, Vicar. As members of the P.C.C. know, I am living in lodgings an awfully long way from the church, and it does make it difficult, now that winter's coming on. I don't really mind, though when I first came a few months ago I was definitely given to understand that there was a small house available for the Assistant Curate. But the main thing is, as you all know, I'm getting married quite soon and I can't possibly stay where I am after that. But I don't want to be the cause of anybody being turned out. So I really don't know what to say."

There was silence again, while all the previous speakers looked at the young man as if he had failed to back them up in their several arguments. A very old woman who had seemed to be asleep said to no one in particular:

"One can't imagine how that dreadful paper could have known."

"He seemed a very pleasant young man," said the Vicar, looking more unhappy than ever. "He listened with real sympathy when I told him, and he said that he only wanted to get the facts so that we wouldn't be misrepresented in any way. And he was quite knowledgeable about ecclesiastical matters, so I'm surprised that he made that solecism about the Good Samaritan."

"He just turned in the story and it was written up by someone else," Overley said impatiently. "It's no good crying over spilt milk. The question is, do we withdraw the notice or don't we? I propose that the matter be put to the vote."

"Yes. Quite. Thank you, churchwarden. Do we withdraw the notice or don't we? I mean, will all those in favour of withdrawing the notice of eviction please signify in the usual manner."

"It seems to be equal," the young priest announced after counting twice.

"Oh dear, what happens now?" asked the Vicar.

"As chairman, you have the casting vote."

"Oh. Well, I'm really very sorry about all the trouble, and I'm sure we shall find a happy solution before my colleague is married. But just for the moment, perhaps we'd better leave things as they are. I will have a talk with the good lady now in occupation and see what can be done. But in view of all this publicity, I think there had better be no actual eviction."

"The situation is quite irregular," Blanch said angrily. "We're only storing up more trouble for ourselves."

"We don't take our orders from the gutter press," said Farrow, redder than ever in spite of the coldness of the room.

"We can afford to learn charity from any source whatever," the Vicar said with surprising firmness. "Miss White, please record that the motion was not carried."

The secretary, a slim woman near middle age but very

attractive in spite of her dull and plain clothes, wrote in the minutes book.

"Now," said the Vicar, "the next and final item on our agenda. The dreadful acts of sacrilege that have taken place since our last meeting. I believe that Mr. Overley has something to say."

Overley got up again and spoke in a low, even voice without the declamatory emphasis with which he had read from the newspaper.

"Unfortunately I can tell little that is not already too well known to this meeting," he said. "The plain facts are that on three occasions in the last month our church has been broken into at night and desecrated. The actual damage has so far been trivial, but the nature of what has been done is horrible to us all. The Reserved Sacrament has twice been stolen from the locked aumbry where it is kept. Obscene words have been written up on the walls of the sanctuary. The altar has been profaned and a very sickening object placed upon it – I need go into no further details. It is clear that we are suffering from the attentions of devotees of some form of Satanism."

"You mean, Black Magic and all that? Nonsense, man. This is the twentieth century." Farrow's moustache bristled as he spoke.

"You echo the words of our journalistic friend. I am sorry to seem old-fashioned, but these things do still go on. We may not believe in witchcraft, but some wretched people still do. You know that I am an antiquarian bookseller. You would be surprised how often I am asked for books giving the secrets of Satanist ritual. No, my dear Farrow, we must accept the fact that we are up against something very nasty indeed."

"It's just wanton vandalism. We ought to get the police on to it," Farrow said.

"With my fellow churchwarden's approval, I have already done so. They seem unable to do much but have promised to refer the matter to Scotland Yard. They at least, unlike some of us here, take the attacks seriously."

"It's a judgement on the Popish practices that are tolerated in this parish."

A sigh ran through the small assembly, and heads turned with a movement of resignation rather than from any need to find out who had spoken. A woman of about forty was standing up in the middle of the second row of chairs, clutching her large black handbag as if she intended to use it as a weapon if she were given any more provocation. She herself, though clearly human in all normal respects, gave the impression of being somehow wrought out of the same black leather. She was thinnish yet seemed to be stuffed until shiny and threadbare with the material for denunciation. Her mouth was a tight clasp, now snapped open for an exodus of tumbling words.

"Ever since I came to live in this parish," she said, "I have watched with sorrow the Protestant church of this land being profaned and degraded. I have sat on this Council and tried to add my voice to the cause of pure religion, in the face of those who are Roman Catholics in all but name. After four hundred years of freedom from superstition and priestcraft, we are being made to bow down before the idols of incense, vestments – and now e hear a word like *aumbry* being used freely in an open ıeeting."

"Aumbries are all right, you know, Miss Mason," the Vicar said gently and more cheerfully. "Of course it depends on what authority you attach to the 1928 Book. And please let me assure you that nobody is expected to bow down to things which are but the traditional externals of Catholic worship."

"Catholic!" said Miss Mason with horrified scorn.

"We so confess ourselves in the Creed," said the Vicar.

"This is just playing with words. I say, look at reality and see where all these practices have brought us. First of all we are held up to public ridicule because of this affair of the parish house, and now we get hooligans treating us with contempt and desecrating the church."

"Our level of churchmanship has nothing to do with the first affair, and I fail to see how it can be affected by the second."

"When people know that a church is riddled with superstition, they see it as a ground for any kind of wickedness. It's as plain as the nose on your face."

The Vicar wiped his sore and insulted nose tenderly and shook his head. Overley put on his scriptural voice and went on talking until Miss Mason sulkily sat down and clicked her mouth shut again.

"As I was saying," Overley continued, "we have asked for the help of the police but they have not yet been able to do anything. They tell us that they are unable to spare men for a permanent watch on the church at night. Mr. Blanch and I therefore want to suggest that some of the male members of this P.C.C. and perhaps others in the parish should arrange to be in the church until these wretches can be caught in the act. It is a dreary and wearying task, but if we do nothing I fear that the next outrage may be much worse."

Ten minutes later, Miss White wrote in her notes for the minutes: "After discussion, Mr. Overley's proposal was accepted and a rota for the coming week was drawn up. There being no further business, the Vicar closed the meeting with prayer at 9.25 p.m."

The councillors rose stiffly from their chairs and stood about in small, awkward groups as if unwilling to exchange the known discomfort for the misery of the open night. A few drifted towards the door and stopped by the stove, which gave no answer to their hopes of a final dole of warmth. The Vicar thrust his sodden handkerchief away and came round the table with the shy kindliness that a lifetime of parish service had not succeeded in disillusioning.

"Something that will interest you, Overley," he said. "I've just got a new load of books – picked them up in a private sale recently. I haven't been through them properly yet but one or two of them are old and might be worth something. Come round and have a look at them one evening."

Overley started a tolerant smile and did not stop it in time to escape the old man's notice.

"I know, my dear fellow," said the Vicar genially. "You think I waste my money by going round on these private chases instead of coming to a respectable bookseller like yourself. Never mind, I don't lay out a great deal, and you've had to admit that I've picked up a rare find once or twice. If I do, the parish will be the better for it when I'm gone. That will cheer your heart, Mr. Farrow."

"I only hope you don't give us the benefit of it for a long time yet, Vicar. We can't do without you so easily." Farrow twitched his moustache and looked awkward.

"Some of you think I'd be worth more to the parish dead than living, and perhaps I should."

"Do you really mean to leave everything to the parish – no other legacies at all?" Blanch asked abruptly. The others all became embarrassed and studied their feet, but Blanch waited with a calm, scholastic interest.

"Where else should it go? There are a few small bequests and one relative to be provided for. The rest belongs to the church I've tried to serve."

"I didn't know you had any family," Blanch persisted.

"There's a nephew. Poor fellow, I'm afraid he hasn't fallen on very easy times. I only hope it may do him some good – I've set aside a fair sum for him. Well, well, you want to get to your homes. Thank you all for coming. I hope our next meeting may bring happier things to discuss."

The Vicar went out and the others followed slowly. The two churchwardens were left together.

"Well, we didn't get much sense out of all that," Blanch said.

"You were on the losing side for once, my dear fellow. I think we've made a lot of progress in the right direction." Overley twirled the key of the door and looked complacent.

"Why on earth did you want to bring up that newspaper rubbish when we nearly had the affair settled?" Blanch asked indignantly. "She couldn't possibly have resisted the order."

"It so happens that I love this grubby little parish of ours, and I don't like to see it held up to scorn and scandal. The position's irregular, I know, but regulations aren't always the best things for a living church. No offence meant."

"I don't suppose the wretched paper will even mention it again now that they've scored a point."

"That's precisely what I hope. We'll get the house in our own time, but I've too much regard for the Vicar to like seeing him driven out of his mind."

"He's half out of it already. The man's good, but he's practically senile. Look at the way he's always carrying on about his will."

"You were very pressing about that tonight, weren't

you? Do you think it was in the best taste?" Overley looked hard at Blanch, who turned away and went to the door.

"He makes me tired," Blanch said without turning his head again. "At every P.C.C. for the last year we've finished up hearing about some addition to his treasures and being assured that it will all go to the parish in the end. I wanted a straight answer out of him, and I got one. Good night."

Outside the Vicar's car could be heard drawing away, after five minutes of tentative and apologetic spluttering. Overley stood looking at the rusty stove.

"If there's money coming, we can certainly find good use for it," he said quietly to the empty room.

A gust brought the rain lashing hard against the windows. Overley put out the lights and went out, carefully locking the door behind him. Then he braced himself against the night and started to walk across the sodden churchyard.

CHAPTER TWO

Two men were sitting in a room high above the Embankment, a room that thousands in London would have envied as an office or even as a home. It was in a building set back from the road and where the continual traffic was heard only as a distant and not unpleasant sound. Its view of the river was magnificent, finest perhaps on a clear autumn day like this one when the low sun made a pool of fire around the barges that fussed their way up or down stream between the bridges. The room was barely furnished and seemed designed for practical efficiency rather than leisurely contemplation of the scene below.

If the two occupants appeared to be indulging in just that contemplation, anyone who knew them well could have told you that they were planning some very practical efficiency indeed. The man who sat at the plain desk was in his late forties, only a little above medium height, with a fair moustache and deceptively soft and gentle blue eyes. His name belied his appearance and his calling, for a trace of Spanish ancestry had endured for generations in the male descent. He was Inspector Herbert Montero and the office was in the C.I.D. section of New Scotland Yard. His companion was tall and thin, with a long, anxious face which tended to flash into clownish humour and return to gravity before anyone was aware of it. Detective Sergeant Jack Springer stood just behind the inspector, looking at the opposite wall and apparently ignoring the file of papers which lay open on the desk.

"Nothing much to go on there, Jack," Montero said after a long silence. "It might be a local job or it might be the beginning of something much bigger. We haven't had a lot of this sort of thing lately, though I remember a case or two years ago when I was in a division."

"Records haven't been able to help us much, sir," Springer agreed sadly. "The only characters nicked for breaking into churches seem to be straight villains – I mean pinching the collection-money and that sort of job. This gang doesn't take anything, just makes a mess and goes off. What do they do it for?"

"That's what we've got to find out. It looks pretty clearly like some fools dabbling in Black Magic. They believe that they can get the greatest power for their tricks by using a church and making a parody of the normal services. Then they like to steal the consecrated bread if there's any about, and use it for their perverted version of the Mass. That ties in with the breaking of the aumbry."

"Oh, yes, one of them. Useful things to have around."

"You're an ignorant copper, Jack, and I despair of you. An aumbry is a kind of wall-cupboard or safe used for reserving the consecrated bread after the communion service.''

"Funny sort of thing to do. This here church, it *is* C. of E., isn't it, sir?''

"Certainly it is, though of the variety that used to be known as 'spiky' when I was young. The virtue of the Church of England is that she manages to suit nearly everybody, like the British Constitution. It's also her weakness of course.''

"But why do they do it?'' Springer asked plaintively. "I mean, these Black Magic characters. What are they after?''

"Different things. Satanists are as mixed in their motives as the rest of us. Some of them believe that they can really give themselves to evil and profit by it – a fallacy, but understandable when you look at the general state of things. For some it's just an excuse for sexual orgies – I suppose they'd say they do it for kicks.''

"What they want are a few kicks up the Khyber Pass, sir. I've heard about them orgies – the popes and cardinals used to have them back in Henry VIII's time. Burning people and all sorts of rotten tricks.''

Montero laughed, then got up and took his raincoat from its peg. He knew that his sergeant tended to put on an act to humour him when a case was difficult, and he still enjoyed it.

"Come on, you true-blue Englishman,'' he said. "We'll go down to the local nick and see if they've anything more for us. I know the super there and that makes it a lot easier to start. Then we'd better look at the church and try to have a word with the Vicar."

"This is a daft sort of job," Springer lamented as he followed his chief.

"Well, you shouldn't have joined. A good copper turns his hand to anything, and this time you'll have to do without the excitement of a murder case."

This was one of the few occasions when Montero's estimate of a case turned out to be wrong.

Benjamin Farrow was in the vestry when the detectives arrived at the church. Being a retired man, he was able to devote a considerable – some would have said a disproportionate–time to the affairs of the parish of which he was treasurer. Like most holders of that responsible and thankless office, he had come to regard the funds of the church as a personal responsibility. He kept up the tradition of honorary treasurers by a great show of despondency at the amount of money in hand and a marked reluctance to admit any expenditure. The parish had a good name in the diocese for financial reliability, if not always for strict adherence to the regulations for worship. The Quota was paid promptly and in full, Farrow regarding this as a kind of insurance against future disaster when diocesan funds might be required for major restoration. The more usual insurances were in good order; the fabric and fittings of the church were fully insured against any contingency including, as is quaintly usual in ecclesiastical policies, acts of God.

Having spent his only exercise of real authority as a very young captain in the last months of the First World War, Farrow had a nostalgic liking for all that represented official order. He greeted Montero and Springer with delight and took them on a tour of the church from boiler-room to belfry. Springer's face grew longer at the sight of the red sanctuary-lamp, the rows of vestments in their several seasonal colours hanging in a cupboard near the vestry, the lingering smell of incense. Montero seemed to be more upset by the hideous wrought-iron screen at the entry to the chancel, the dull pitchpine pews, the deep-coloured stained-glass windows with fulsome dedications; and it was perhaps the quality of the pictures rather than the implied practice which made him wince on passing the successive Stations of the Cross. The church had been built at the height of the neo-gothic revival and had suffered preservation as older churches had suffered unhappy restoration.

After they had been shown the rota of voluntary watchers and assured Farrow that everything possible would be done, they withdrew in search of the nearest pub that sold sandwiches. Springer produced a harrowing cough and made pointed remarks about the smoky atmosphere until the inspector silenced him with a glance.

Farrow went back into the vestry and resumed his work on the accounts. After a time, making sure that there was no one in the church, he opened a drawer in the table where he was working, took out an old service revolver and held it lovingly in the position to fire.

Sarah White had been secretary to the P.C.C. for a much shorter time than Farrow had been treasurer, but she was already regarded as a permanent feature of P.C.C. meetings. On the evening of the day when Montero had begun his investigations, she came into the church and knelt in a back pew. The need for prayer was great in her but she was unable to fix her mind on any devotion. Her eyes kept wandering towards the figure who sat with bowed head in the aisle at the farther end of the church. It looked as if the Vicar was waiting to hear someone's confession: that was the place for it, the place where perhaps she ought to be at that moment. She suddenly longed for the familiar feel of the low kneeling-desk under her elbows, the sight of the crucifix above, the low voice of the old priest sitting beside her, his hand hiding his face from the human recognition that might turn comfort into shame. She stayed still for a few minutes then went out without looking towards the confessional again.

Phillip Overley always enjoyed the walk to the church from his flat over the bookshop. It was far enough to stretch the muscles and give time for some preliminary meditation, but not too far to become a burden on wet nights or cold early mornings. There was a church nearer at hand, but the boundary of its parish fell just short of where he lived, and he was a believer in worshipping where he officially belonged. Besides, and perhaps more important to him, he liked the level of churchmanship and was impatient of the plainer services offered at the nearer place. In his years as vicar's warden he had become fond of the old priest; the forgetfulness and ignorance of regulations which infuriated some of the congregation seemed unimportant compared with the tender pastoral devotion, the dignity of public worship.

There was not any particular reason for going to the church this evening, but he liked to spend a few minutes there to satisfy himself that all was in order. A bachelor, with a life not extending far beyond the buying and selling of the old books that he loved, he found a greater satisfaction than he would admit to himself in the name of an official position. It was something, in the great anonymity of London life, to belong somewhere, to be a recognised figure with rights and duties plainly laid down. He could slip into his special pew where the churchwarden's staff stood in its socket, and assume a new role as if fitting on an actor's mask.

That affair of the house was troublesome, he reflected as he walked through the dark evening, clouded with the threat of fog after an unusually warm day. Coming together with these beastly acts of sacrilege, it laid a heavy responsibility on the parish officers. He had already kept one vigil in the church without success. What on earth were the police doing about it? He frowned in his prim way, deploring the burden of a position which he was determined not to relinquish.

Overley had his own key, but the church was usually kept open until well into the evening and he was able to walk straight in. Despite the attacks, the Vicar had refused to depart from his practice of keeping the building open as long as possible for those who might want to come in and sit or pray. It was an active parish, and it was rare to find the place deserted at any reasonable hour. He pushed open the door and then stood aside to let Sarah White come out. She took no notice of him but went past with her head down and her body tense. What was wrong with her, he wondered. The whole parish seemed to be getting afflicted with troubles of one kind or another. He breathed the incense-smelling air and felt happier.

An old man dozed in a pew, one of the derelicts who haunted the church for shelter from the colder evenings. Ought he to be turned out? It was the churchwardens' duty to keep the church free from scandal and profanation. Overley smiled bitterly: a tired tramp was little to bear on top of press publicity and Satanism. The Vicar would have thought first of charity, and rightly. Overley looked at the vested figure sitting at the confessional, and felt a surge of affectionate pity for the frailty that had to sort out the sins of those who were even frailer. Surely it wasn't one of the Vicar's regular times for confession, though? Overley went and looked at the typed notice in the porch and verified that it was not. Some special penitent then, perhaps a first confession that was likely to take a long time. There was no trespassing on this duty: business would have to wait.

Overley genuflected with precision, turned and went quietly out of the church.

CHAPTER THREE

"I couldn't exactly hear the words that he was saying, but I'm quite sure that they were Latin."

Miss Lucinda Mason nodded her head vigorously to emphasise the horror of the Vicar's latest offence. Her guest took another valiant gulp at his cup of powdered coffee and condensed milk and looked sympathetically shocked. Angus Sprott was devoted to the society of which he was the permanent paid secretary, but he occasionally found some of the members a bit difficult. The society itself was dated in foundation by its title of the 'League for Confuting and Suppressing the Errors of the Tractarians', but it continued to flourish and to find work to do. Its methods were correct and peaceful: not for them the interruption of services or the tearing down of church notices. But wherever the dreadful suspicion of Romish practice was whispered to be tainting the Church of England, Angus Sprott was quickly on the scene – writing to the church papers, seeking interviews with the Bishop, eloquent in godly remonstrance with the offending clergyman. A stout upholder of the Prayer Book, he tended to censor in his own usage its mention of priests and dangerous words like confession and absolution.

A parish like this one seemed always beyond hope of remedy until Lucinda Mason came on the scene. Upholding her right and duty to worship in her parish church and not to seek one more suitable to her tastes, she was an elected member of the P.C.C. within a few months of her arrival in the district. Gathering to her support the few staunchly protestant worshippers, together with those who disliked other members of the P.C.C. enough to elect anyone who would be guaranteed to make them uncomfortable, she soon became the spokeswoman of all the discontented elements in the congregation. We have heard one of her outbursts, a fair specimen of those which she was liable to reproduce without regard to the subject under discussion. She faithfully attended the principal services, standing while others knelt and kneeling while they stood, keeping her hands as firmly from the Sign of the Cross as the Catechism instructed her to keep them from picking and stealing. Now, armed with a list of iniquities, she had summoned Angus Sprott to drink what passed for coffee and to take counsel with her.

"A very unhappy affair," Sprott said. "As you know, I have spoken with the Vicar on more than one occasion but without moving him. I fear that his heart is hardened. Such a charming old gentleman too – a pity that he should be a Romaniser."

"His charm deceives too many people," Miss Mason retorted. "You and I know that a smile can lie directly over a black heart."

Sprott looked thoughtful at this piece of anatomy and went on quickly to talk about the latest troubles in the parish. He agreed with Miss Mason that superstitious practices were a positive encouragement to sacrilege. He was less inclined to see theological significance in the letting of the parish house, but Miss Mason was firm.

"A minister who is unfaithful in one point will be unfaithful in all," she declared. "If he defies the law of the land in his conduct of services, will he heed it in matters of rents and leases? It's my belief that he's lining his own pockets over that house."

"Come, come, Miss Mason. We must be careful not to make accusations that may be unjustified, or else we shall lose our main point of advantage. I really don't think he's dishonest in that way. Besides, I understand that he has quite a considerable private income beyond his stipend."

"And where does he get it? Everybody knows that he's quite a rich man. I believe he's been making money out of the Church all the years of his ministry."

"I really don't think we ought to suggest that. Is it not true that he has made a will leaving it all to the parish funds?"

"Most of it, so he says, except for some wretched nephew or other. Why, unless he came by it dishonestly? It's a typically Popish trick to try to save himself from perdition."

"I do think we ought to be careful, Miss Mason. We

have quite enough cause for action on matters which can be proved. I came into the church for a few minutes on my way here – a sorry sight in every way. Unfortunately, there seemed to be very little that was positively illegal. We must tread warily."

"The man ought to be prosecuted," Miss Mason said firmly.

"It's so difficult to get convictions nowadays. I fear that things have got very lax in the past fifty years. Our countrymen don't seem to realise what a precious birthright they are selling. Things haven't been the same since the Roman hierarchy was restored."

"Will you advise the League to take action or not? If you don't, I shall stand on my rights as a parishioner and delate him to the Bishop."

"You are a wonderful worker for the truth, Miss Mason. Just let me have another talk with him – a word in season may still prevail. But perhaps not tonight, since the Vicarage is a long way and I have other calls to make. No, thank you so much, I won't indulge in another cup of your excellent coffee."

The Vicarage was in fact rather a long way. The old one had stood close to the church but had been destroyed by bombing which left the church itself almost untouched. The house which was eventually acquired for the Vicar was at the other end of the straggling London parish, a good ten minutes' walk away. Miss Mason was fortunate in lodging almost directly behind the church itself, so Sprott had a fair excuse for not making the journey and also for hinting for the hundredth time that the League ought to let him have an allowance for a car.

The New Vicarage, as some of the older parishioners still called it, was far from being a new house. Built towards the end of the last century, it was one of the few in that district which was still used for single occupation and not divided into flats. The Vicar found it too large and inconvenient, the Diocesan Board of Finance heard frequent grumbles about the rates and upkeep, but the house continued to serve its ecclesiastical purpose. On this particular evening it looked even less attractive than usual. The threatened fog had turned into a general dampness, an oozing and dripping that refused to become a real downpour and get itself over. The front gate was slimy to the touch, the path was slippery with neglected fallen leaves, and the double-fronted house was like a dark bulk that had somehow drifted up on the weather and been stranded.

Mrs. Acres scarcely noticed these things. The years of acting as the Vicar's housekeeper had brought familiarity with every aspect of the house and its surroundings. Only the sudden absence of minor inconveniences and discomforts would have made her senses alert. On this occasion, her mind was agreeably occupied with other matters, such as the cinema she had been to, the prospect of a strong cup of tea and some favourite biscuits in her own room, the pleasant sense that the Vicar's supper things need not be washed up until the morning.

"If he's remembered to eat anything at all," she murmured to herself, diving into her handbag for her key as she gained the shelter of the glazed porch. Then she suddenly gave a little shriek and jumped with agility remarkable in her years and general shape.

"I'm sorry, Mrs. Acres, did I alarm you?"

"Oh, Mr. Malving, it's you. I wondered who it was, standing there like that."

The young clergyman who had been the centre of concern at the P.C.C. meeting came forward until the light from the street lamp showed him more clearly. He was wearing a dark raincoat, buttoned up so that his clerical collar was covered, and a rather disreputable cap, so it was not surprising that Mrs. Acres had failed to see him as he stood back in the shadow of the porch. Now he pulled off his cap and spoke with the diffident but firm tone that was already well known to the regular congregation.

"I've been waiting for some time," he said. "I'd arranged to see the Vicar, but I couldn't get any answer when I arrived. Do you know whether he's in?"

"Well, he ought to be, if he's expecting you. I've been out since half past five, so I couldn't say."

Mrs. Acres did not share the common enthusiasm about Malving; she considered that he gave himself airs beyond his station, for she had a firm sense of the hierarchy proper within a parish. When the young man came to years of discretion and had a parish of his own, that would be time enough for him to express opinions. As it was, he tended to be too free in his ideas of what folk old enough to be his mother ought to be doing with their lives. All this, and more, ran in a confused stream of disapproval through her mind as they stood together and swallowed the damp air with its smell of leaves.

"I've rung the bell several times, but nothing happened," Malving said with a look of innocence that had no effect on Mrs. Acres.

"Well, he must have gone out. I suppose he was called away to someone sick, and I'll be surprised if he gave himself a bite to eat before he went."

The crunch of gravel accompanied by a forced cough made them both turn quickly. Benjamin Farrow, also suitably buttoned against the weather, came round the side of the house and looked apologetic.

"I thought I heard voices," he said. "I've just been round to see if the Vicar was in his study since I couldn't get an answer at the front. There's a light in his window, and I tapped on the pane, but the curtains were drawn. I wanted to have a word with him about the accounts."

"How long have you been waiting?" Malving asked.

"About five minutes I suppose, Father," Farrow said.

"Funny, I didn't hear you or see you go round."

"If it comes to that, I didn't see you either, Father."

This time Farrow seemed to give the title a sarcastic tone.

"You couldn't have come to this door – I've been here for ages."

"Well, we must have missed each other. Why don't we all go in and wait?"

Farrow's military tone succeeded in producing a key and some muttered grumble from Mrs. Acres, who opened the door and then turned as if to send the two men away. Then she wailed and ran off to the basement stairs, up which a distinct smell of burning was drifting. Malving and Farrow took advantage of her distress and followed.

"I knew it – I knew the dear man couldn't be trusted to get his bit of supper out of the oven. Now he's had nothing to eat, and my lovely cottage pie's burnt to a cinder."

"Well, never mind, Mrs. Acres," Malving said in tones of consolation. "The Vicar has probably been giving his mind to some task that needed all his attention. We shall be the richer for it in due course."

The curate's pastoral care was cut short by a startling military oath that made him turn with a pained expression. Farrow had gone down the corridor to the Vicar's study, tapped twice on the door and then opened it. Now he was standing with an expression on his face which made Malving hurry to join him. The Vicar was sitting in his customary chair, turned half away from his desk to face the room. He had fallen over one side so that the upper part of his body was supported by the surface of the desk, along which his right arm was stretched out.

Malving gave an exclamation under his breath, whether pious or profane was never revealed, pushed past Farrow and went and raised the Vicar's head. There was blood on the front of the old man's cassock, down to his feet and on the old sheepskin rug.

"Is he dead?" Farrow asked sharply.

"He's been murdered." Malving spoke in a decisive way now, with no hint of diffidence. "He was writing when it happened."

He pointed to a pen clutched between the fingers of the Vicar's right hand. Then he bent and peered at what lay beneath it. A large desk-diary was opened at that day's date. There were a number of entries in the neat, old-fashioned writing that he had come to know well as the Vicar's. Then, scrawled so as to be almost illegible, came a short phrase. "Re July 23," Malving read aloud. The second figure tailed off into a line that ran over the edge of the page and pointed to the lifeless hand, the clutched pen.

Now Mrs. Acres was at the door and Farrow, strangely gentle, was trying to keep her from entering the study. Malving stood upright and looked at both of them with authority, as if he felt the weight of the parish suddenly come upon him.

"We must get the police here at once," he said. "I'm afraid it's too late for anyone else to be of use."

The three of them stood in a tableau of amazement

for a few seconds that seemed endless. Then a voice from behind made them all start and turn quickly. Two men were just inside the front door, one of them tall and thin, the other shorter but firm and efficient in his manner.

"Good evening," the second man said, while his tall companion gazed with big melancholy eyes. "Excuse my walking in, but the door was open and there didn't seem to be anyone about. I am Detective Inspector Montero of the Metropolitan C.I.D. I arranged to see the Vicar this evening – do you know if he's in?"

"The Vicar's in here." Malving pointed into the study and waited for the two detectives to come forward. For a moment, he looked almost as if he was amused.

CHAPTER FOUR

It has already been mentioned that Cyril Blanch, the people's warden, was a scholarly-looking man. He was perhaps fortunate in this, for he was a university lecturer and the distinction of appearance is not one shared by all the profession. While these unhappy events were taking place at the Vicarage, he was sitting in a flat on the other side of London, drinking port with his colleague Adam Ludlow. Blanch taught mathematics, a subject uncomprehended and distrusted by Ludlow, whose field was English. Nevertheless, the two men were on friendly terms and occasionally spent an evening together. Although not very high in the ranking of his college, Ludlow had a reputation for various idiosyncrasies that made him a well-known and somewhat admired member of the Senior Common Room. He had more than once got himself mixed up in a case of murder and arrived at its solution through curious methods of his own, and he was also known to be full of odd bits of knowledge which might or might not be connected with his subject. It was for the second of these reasons that Blanch had now sought his company.

Blanch sat upright in his armchair, clutching his glass

tightly and looking as if he was about to conclude some very valuable business deal. Ludlow was sprawled almost horizontally, his long legs taking up a considerable part of the floor. His tweed suit was already so creased that it scarcely mattered if a few more wrinkles were added. His grey eyes looked reposeful under their bushy brows, but he was watching his visitor with keen appraisal. His hands were clasped in a manner well known and privately imitated by some of his own students. His glass of port was laid on one side of his chair, his half-smoked pipe on the other. The room was a proliferation of books and papers in which the two men seemed to be suspended like floating islands.

"The fact is," Blanch was saying, "that the man simply can't be trusted. He's continually mislaying things because he's so hopelessly untidy and absent-minded. I told him only the other day that he ought to make written notes of where he puts things."

"Very regrettable," Ludlow agreed. "One feels sorry for a man who can't keep his things in good order. It would be intolerable to live without being able to put a hand on something immediately it was wanted."

He gestured amply at the chaos around him and looked very pleased with himself.

"He's a good man, mind you," Blanch went on. "Something of a saint in his way, but even saints are liable to get senile and need looking after. It's nothing to me one way or the other, but I don't want the parish to be the ultimate loser. Heaven knows, we could do with the money when it comes."

"Let me be sure I understand your meaning," Ludlow said, using a phrase that he is fond of saying to students whose essays are particularly ill-written. "You are concerned lest the Vicar should somehow lose the books that he has just bought and which you think may be valuable. Since a large part of his not inconsiderable personal fortune is destined to come to the parish after his death, you would be failing in your duty as a churchwarden if you did not make strenuous efforts to safeguard the legacy. Do I describe the situation accurately?"

Blanch nodded, too concerned with his problem to wonder whether Ludlow was being at all sarcastic.

"The point is," he said, "that I don't know whether these books are worth anything or not. I believe the old chap's picked up some rare finds once or twice, but he also collects a lot of rubbish. That's where I'd like you to help. You know about such things, and I'd be the first to admit that I don't."

"I have a certain interest in these matters," said Ludlow, looking pleased again.

"And you'd say it's possible to get rare books cheaply in a sale?"

"The hope of making exciting discoveries is fainter than it used to be," Ludlow said. "The dealers seldom miss an auction, and practically every old book has a precisely known market value. It's all a very regrettable

symptom of that society which some people are inclined to regard as progressive. Wilde said that a cynic
is a man who knows the price of everything and the
value of nothing, and I should apply that epigram with
deep feeling —"

"But it is possible," Blanch almost shouted, not the
first of Ludlow's colleagues to attempt to interrupt
him in full digression.

"Oh, yes, it's possible. An old book may have lain
for centuries in an attic – a book cheap and common
when it was bought and then preserved by chance
while the other copies were used and discarded. If the
ultimate owner is careless and knows nothing of these
things, a valuable book or manuscript may be put in a
bundle with others of no worth and sold collectively for
a low price. I have little expectation of ever getting rich
that way, though I have had one or two exciting discoveries. One never knows. After all, we owe almost all
the poetry of Thomas Traherne to the chance discovery
of a manuscript —"

"That's what I thought," said Blanch, interrupting
again. "So if the Vicar has got hold of anything valuable,
you could persuade him to look after it properly – deposit it somewhere or get a good price for it. Otherwise,
he's likely to read it once and throw it into the next
jumble sale."

Ludlow is always ready to go and look at old books,
and he never minds giving an opinion. After another
glass of port, the two men went and got into Blanch's

car and drove off across London. Blanch was feeling distinctly pleased with himself. He was going to show that he had the interests of the parish at heart as much as some other people who needn't be named. And if it happened that the Vicar had made a good purchase, how very nice it would be to point it out to him before Overley came along with his expert knowledge.

When they drew up outside the Vicarage, both of them were surprised to see several windows lit up, the front door ajar and two cars standing in the road outside. One of these was an official police car, and the other looked vaguely familiar to Ludlow; it must be added that his awareness of cars is vague at the best of times. When they reached the porch, a uniformed policeman barred their way and politely asked them their business.

"We have called to see the Vicar. I am a church-warden of this parish," Blanch said with dignity. "What is happening?"

"All callers have to be reported to the inspector in charge," the constable said. He turned and called down the corridor that there were two gentlemen at the door.

"Ask them to wait a minute," a voice floated back. Ludlow started with surprise when he heard it.

It was Springer's turn to look surprised when he emerged from the study and saw Ludlow, whose tendency to get himself mixed up with murders had several times aroused mingled respect and exasperation in the official investigators. Ludlow always enjoys being the centre of attraction and he was pleased to see the effect on his colleague Blanch when Montero came out and greeted him with a warmth only slightly tempered by suspicion at his being there at all. Since Montero and Ludlow have a habit of falling into literary exchanges when they are together, it was a few minutes before Springer was able to recall his superior to the more urgent business and explain what had happened.

The resources even of the large Vicarage were being strained by Montero's attempt to keep his witnesses in different rooms until he had talked to them. Blanch was asked to wait, and Ludlow was admonished to behave himself if he wanted to be allowed to stay – an injunction which he received with silent reproach and a look of innocence. In the drawing-room at the front of the house, incongruously amid faded chintz and coffee-tables, Montero began his interviews by calling in a tearful Mrs. Acres.

Between sniffs, she explained that she had gone out at half past five, leaving the Vicar's supper to cook slowly in the oven. She had been at the cinema and come straight back.

"Which cinema did you go to?" Montero asked.

"The Redplush, in Finchley."

"Some distance from here. How did you get there?"

"I took a bus – well, two buses because you have to change. But I specially wanted to see the film there."

"I see. What's the name of it?"

"It was called 'Passion and Shame' – it's only just been released. You must have read the reviews in the papers." Mrs. Acres blushed deeper than her already reddened eyes.

"Did you go with anyone? Or perhaps you met someone who knew you?"

"No. But I've got the half of my ticket."

She fished in the handbag that she had been clutching ever since she came into the house, and produced the stub of a cinema ticket. Without seeming to give it more than a quick glance, Springer wrote the serial number in his notebook.

"We've no reason to doubt your word, Mrs. Acres," Montero said. "You say that the Vicar's supper was in the oven, so presumably you did not expect him to go very far this evening."

"He didn't say whether he was going out or not. He often goes to the church early in the evening when people drop in on their way home from work. Oh dear, that's not true now, is it? The poor man won't ever go there again."

She wailed loudly while the two detectives made encouraging noises and looked embarrassed.

"It wasn't one of his evenings for hearing confessions," Mrs. Acres resumed at last, freshly voluble after her distress. "And he didn't have anything in his diary for this evening."

"So you don't think he was expecting any callers?"

"People were always coming round about something –
to get a form signed, or help with their pensions, or
asking for money. That's apart from all the parish
business. He'd never turn anyone away, no matter
how tired he was. I used to say he was his own worst
enemy, but he'd never let me say he was out if he
wasn't."

"Did he always write down appointments in his
diary?"

"He had to, because of his poor memory. Sometimes
he'd even forget to put it in, and there'd be a mix-up,
but he usually got it right. But when he got interested
in something like those old books of his, time meant
nothing. He'd forget to eat his meals if I didn't keep
calling him – like he never had that good cottage pie
this evening."

"So there was nothing significant in the fact that it
was uneaten. Would you say that he could easily have
forgotten about it even if nothing had happened to
prevent or worry him?"

After Mrs. Acres had agreed, and had been allowed to
sniff herself back to her own quarters, Montero looked
through the notes which Springer handed to him and
sighed deeply.

"Nothing much there," he said. "She had nothing to
gain from his death but unemployment, as far as we
know. Of course, she had every opportunity. Check up
on that ticket tomorrow, though there's no way of
proving that she didn't just go in and come out after a

few minutes. But I don't think we need waste much time with Mrs. Acres."

"I thought she was a bit too slick producing the ticket before she was asked," Springer said.

"Maybe. Now let's have the Curate and see what he can tell us."

Malving was by no means the image of the traditional nervous curate when Springer ushered him in. He seemed to have gained strength in the last hour, as if the shock of violent death had matured him. In reply to Montero's questions, he said that he had arrived at the Vicarage precisely at eight o'clock, on the scooter which he always used. Getting no reply to his rings, he had waited in the porch. Mrs. Acres had arrived at half past eight.

"It was a long wait," Montero said. "Was it essential to see the Vicar this evening?"

"Well, it was rather important."

"What were you doing in the earlier part of the evening?"

"I had a few visits to make around the parish, and I was at the hospital until nearly half past seven. Then I called in at the church for a few minutes to see that everything was in order for early celebration tomorrow morning. Then I came straight here."

"Was there anyone in the church?"

"No. Well, one old sort of tramp who spends a lot of time there and does no harm. I had to turn him out because it was time to lock up."

"You've been having a bit of trouble there recently, I believe. In fact, that's why we were here at all this evening. Was there talk of people keeping guard at night?"

"Yes, the churchwardens have arranged a rota, but they don't come on until quite late when there aren't many people about in the street. These horrible outrages seem to have occurred mostly in the small hours of the morning."

"Was the Vicar expecting you this evening?" Springer asked suddenly on getting a quick nod from the inspector.

"Oh – well, yes – yes, he was."

"What were you going to talk about?"

"Parish matters – you know, the usual sort of routine stuff."

"Would you say he had a good memory for keeping appointments?"

"Shockingly bad, I'm afraid. That's why I wasn't unduly surprised when he didn't seem to be in. I just settled down to wait until he came back."

"There is no entry in his diary about your coming," Montero said. "I understood that he wrote down everything. Are you quite sure that he was expecting you?"

"Well – that is – I meant he was always expecting me. I mean, one was liable to drop in any old time."

"I see. So that means that the matters you wanted to discuss were of your choosing rather than his?"

"In a way, yes."

"Would you like to tell me what you had in mind?"

"I'd rather not. It was a private matter. Do I have to tell you?"

"We have neither the means nor the desire to compel you, Mr. Malving. If you don't choose to tell us, we may draw our own conclusions from your silence and from the fact that you were prepared to wait indefinitely on a rather unpleasant evening."

Malving shifted uncomfortably but said nothing. Montero did not press the question but turned to another one as if there had been no difficulty.

"Would you say that the Vicar had any enemies?" he asked. Malving shook his head.

"He was loved by everybody. He'd been over forty years in this parish, and he seemed to know all the people here, whether they came to church or not. It isn't easy to become really well known and respected in London, but he did. Of course, there were differences of opinion over parish matters. I think some of the laymen were impatient with him sometimes, but there was no real hostility. He wasn't the sort of man you could hate."

"Somebody hated him though – or stood to gain by his death," Montero said grimly.

Benjamin Farrow was called in next, truculent at being kept waiting but soon calmed by Montero's famous blend of tact and firmness. The inspector discovered that Farrow had been in the parish almost as long as the Vicar and was proud of his knowledge of parish affairs.

"Would you mind telling me what you did this evening, from about six?" Montero asked eventually.

"Well, I was at home all afternoon and early evening – my wife can vouch for that. We had an early supper and then I came round here soon after eight. It was just on quarter past when I arrived."

"How did you come?"

"I walked. I don't live far away and I like to keep up some exercise. It's easy to let yourself slip when you retire."

"Was the Vicar expecting you?"

"No, but it was quite usual for me to call in if something cropped up in the church finances. It was an excuse for a stroll, whether he was in or not."

"But this evening you thought it worth waiting. Your business must have been very pressing."

"Not particularly. But when I couldn't get an answer, I went round to the back where he had his study. There was a light there and I tapped on the window. I got puzzled and a bit alarmed when there was no reply, so I came back to the front and found young Malving there."

"That was nearly half past eight. Surely you didn't stand at the back of the house for fifteen minutes?"

"I suppose time just went."

"I suppose it did. Did you see Mr. Malving when you went to the front door for the first time?"

"No, I didn't."

"Did you go to the front at all – or straight to the back?" Springer shot at him suddenly.

"Of course I went to the front. What are you suggesting?"

"Mr. Malving says he was there for half an hour," Springer pressed. Farrow shrugged his shoulders and muttered inaudibly.

"I haven't yet got the doctor's report," Montero said, "but my own very superficial examination suggested that the Vicar had been shot through the heart by a heavy revolver."

He leaned back and looked at the ceiling as if it would answer him. The effect of his remark on Farrow was remarkable, producing strangled gulps and a redder face than ever.

"I just wondered whether, with your wide knowledge of the parish and its people, you knew who owned such a weapon? Perhaps an old service revolver," Montero went on, suddenly switching his calm blue eyes from the ceiling to look full at Farrow, who stammered that he did not.

"When you spoke to Mr. Malving the *second* time you went to the front door," Springer said with heavy emphasis, "did he say why he wanted to see the Vicar?"

"No." Farrow stopped trembling and looked cunningly pleased to change the subject. "But I'll bet it was about the parish house. He was really upset about losing his chance of it."

So Montero learned all about the letting of the house, the arguments at the P.C.C. and the fact that Malving had been disgruntled ever since the decision not to press for eviction of the present tenants. All this left the detectives thoughtful and not displeased.

"He was properly upset about the revolver," Springer said admiringly after the treasurer had gone. "How did you know to ask him, sir?"

"For once, my question was quite innocent. He looked the sort of man who might know, and he obviously does. We'll be talking to him again, and we'll get a good check of those accounts he's been keeping. But just now we'd better see the gentleman who deposited Mr. Ludlow in our laps so unexpectedly."

Cyril Blanch looked calm and benign enough, and anxious to help. He explained about the books and how he had brought Ludlow over in the hope of getting a look at them.

"Mr. Ludlow is a friend of yours, is he?" Montero asked.

"Well – I know him as a colleague," Blanch replied, not sure whether Ludlow's acquaintance with the police was to his credit or not.

"Yes, I imagine one could hardly miss him in any community. As it turned out, he never got a look at the books. Do you know where the Vicar was keeping them?"

"I've no idea – that's just it, they might be anywhere and now we shan't know."

"Do you mean that he'd hide them away somewhere like a dog does a bone?" Springer asked bluntly.

"Yes, that's about it. He used to leave valuable

things lying around anywhere, and we kept warning him that they might be stolen or accidentally damaged. So more recently he's taken to stowing his new purchases away in the most unlikely places of safety. Only last summer he put some things in the stove in the vestry rooms, and they nearly got burned when the verger went to light it for the first time in the autumn. Since then, I believe he started writing down a reminder of where he'd put things."

"But you don't know whether he'd done that with his latest purchase?"

"I've no idea."

"Would you say he had any enemies?" Montero asked.

"I can't think of any. He was really a very lovable old man, though his eccentricities could be a bit irritating at times. As one of the churchwardens, I was forced to criticise him from time to time, but I always have had the greatest regard for him as a priest."

"Ah yes, I remember your name now as one of the two gentlemen who first got in touch with the local police about these acts of sacrilege in the church."

"That's right, Inspector. Overley and I reported the affair. I do hope that you'll find the culprits soon."

"We shall do our best, sir. But I'm afraid we're going to have more serious business to occupy us for the time being."

"I can think of nothing more serious than vandalism in the House of God," Blanch said sternly.

"You may be right, and I wouldn't presume to argue with you, but the law as it stands puts a higher rate on murder. You might be wise to keep up your own system of guard for the present, though we'll try to keep the church under observation. By the way, who's due there tonight?"

Blanch pulled out a pocket book and consulted it.

"Good gracious," he exclaimed, "I am. I'd quite forgotten with all this frightful business. I ought to get along soon."

"We needn't keep you any longer. Probably we shall want to talk to you again."

Montero returned to the study. The Vicar's body had been removed but plain-clothes men were busy with cameras and fingerprint equipment. In the middle of the activity, Ludlow was sitting happily by the fire reading the Vicar's desk-diary.

"What the devil are you doing here? Why did you let him in?" Montero asked sharply.

"He said you'd sent him to have a look round, sir. I thought he must be some expert you'd called in to help," said one of the detectives.

Ludlow looked up from his reading with pained innocence.

"I said nothing of the kind," he retorted. "I may have murmured something about being glad to help, and that I had often worked with you in the past, but I laid no claim to special privilege. These men kindly allowed me to rest here and read to pass the time."

Montero turned to Blanch, who was standing aimlessly in the corridor.

"You'd better forget about your vigil tonight," he said. "Take Mr. Ludlow back to his flat before I do something I might regret."

CHAPTER FIVE

The police surgeon was short and inclined to stoutness, and he continually smoked the cigarettes whose lethal effect on other people was one of his articles of faith.

"He was killed between six-thirty and seven-thirty," he told Montero some time after Ludlow had been sent home in disgrace. "He was shot in the chest, the bullet just missing the heart but getting near enough to finish him off. If you want it in technical terms, it's all down in the written report. Death was almost instantaneous."

"You can't put the time of death any more precisely?" Montero asked, stifling a yawn and thinking of his bed.

"It's not so easy as you laymen suppose," the doctor grumbled. "In this case it's complicated by the fact that he'd eaten nothing for hours before he was killed, so the stomach was empty. Also there was a blazing fire in the room to keep up the body temperature. After making all allowances, I'm not going to take an oath on anything more definite. He wasn't alive after seven-thirty, that's certain. Poor fellow, he was a good man whatever you may or may not think of his profession. I saw a lot of him – especially when he'd taken over after I could do no more."

"Would he have been able to write anything after he was shot?" Montero asked. "You've seen the scrawl on his diary – what do you think?"

"I should expect him to have lost consciousness immediately and died in a few seconds. But people don't always behave according to the books, and I've known a few odd things to happen when there was no apparent conscious control. He did write something, and you can make what you like of it."

Montero and Springer came out into the late night, still dripping without positive rain. Several policemen, some uniformed and some in plain clothes, were methodically searching the garden. Springer's keen eyes gleamed; he gripped Montero's arm and pointed to an empty flower bed under the front window. A trail of deep, clear footprints led from the window towards the side of the house and disappeared on the gravel path. Montero knelt and examined the prints briefly, then gave a deep sigh, got up and looked round sternly.

"Which of you has been walking across here?" he asked.

"I'm afraid I did, sir," said a young man in a belted raincoat.

Springer made condemnatory noises with his tongue but Montero looked almost benevolently at the offending detective.

"How long have you been with us now, Arcott?" he asked.

"Five months, sir."

"How long were you on the beat in uniform?"

"Nearly six years, sir."

"Quite so. There's always a shortage of uniformed men, you know. Your old division would probably be glad to have you back at any time."

With a kindly smile, he went out of the front gate and got into the car that had brought them on a very different errand so many hours before.

In spite of Montero's late departure from the Vicarage, he was making the bell ring in Overley's bookshop as he pushed the door open at an early hour the following morning. Overley emerged, looking surprised to have a customer so soon. It was a small shop, its meagre floorspace reduced to a few square feet by the books that stood on shelves, were piled on tables and overflowed on to every flat surface. It seemed unlikely that anyone could know what books there were in stock, still less find any of them. However, Overley was fully in command of his business and was not a man given to making mistakes.

"We would have been coming to see you today in any case, about the offences committed in the church," Montero said after introducing himself. "As it turned out, we've got a more serious affair to deal with. I was wondering whether you saw the Vicar at any time yesterday evening – after five-thirty, when the housekeeper went out."

"He was in the church soon after seven, but I don't know for how long."

"Was he indeed? Did you speak to him?"

"No, I wasn't able to. I walked down to the church as I often do in the evening. Since these beastly attacks started, I've tried to look in more often – though nothing's likely to happen so early, but you can imagine how one feels. The Vicar was sitting in the confessional corner when I went in, so of course I couldn't go and disturb him. I didn't stay long."

"Does that mean that you particularly wanted to speak to him about something?"

"Oh no. I'd certainly have passed a word or two with him if he'd been free, that's all I meant."

"There was someone making his confession, was there?"

"No. The Vicar was obviously waiting for someone to come, though it wasn't one of his regular times. It must have been a special arrangement."

"Was there anyone else in the church at all?"

"Sarah White was just coming out as I went in – she's the secretary of the P.C.C. No one else, except an old fellow who spends a lot of time there. He seemed to be asleep."

"Did you speak to Miss White?" Springer said, looking very disapproving at all this talk of confessions.

"No, she seemed to be in a hurry. In fact, she was looking very worried about something and didn't seem to recognize me. Could you tell me what all this is about, please? You spoke of a more serious affair. What has happened?"

Montero told him. Overley went pale and swayed as if he was about to fall. Springer took his arm in a practised grip and lowered him to a chair after sweeping some valuable volumes to the floor. Overley held his head in his hands for a while, then straightened up and crossed himself with a grand gesture that shocked Springer even more.

"May he rest in peace," Overley said. "Forgive me, Inspector, but this has been a terrible surprise. To think that I saw him such a short time before he was killed. Who in the world can have done such a thing?"

"That is what we intend to find out, sir."

"I'll do anything I can to help you. I was extremely fond of him, you know. Forgetful and eccentric he certainly was, but there was a goodness that made it all seem unimportant. He didn't have a single real enemy."

"He had at least one. And that one either possessed or was able to get hold of a heavy revolver. Can you help us there at all?"

"Farrow!" Overley shouted the name and jumped up. "So he killed him. But why, Inspector, why did he do it?"

"We don't yet know that he did, Mr. Overley. Can you explain a little more fully what you mean?"

"I'm sorry. I've no right to make an accusation like that." Overley walked about as far as the limited space allowed, beating his hands together. "All I know is that

Farrow has a gun – a service revolver that he's kept ever since the First World War, I believe. Apparently he's kept it cleaned and loaded all these years. It's an extraordinary thing to do. Sometimes I think that he was never really happy except when he was in uniform and able to carry arms. Does that make sense to you?"

"Only too much sense. Some of these sentimental attachments to old weapons have led to a lot of trouble before. But how do you know all this?"

"When the outrages in the church started and we decided to have a rota of men keeping watch, Farrow said that he intended to keep his gun ready to deal with any intruders. He brought it into the vestry when it was his turn for duty, and as far as I know he left it there. I wouldn't touch a thing like that."

"How many people knew about this?"

"The whole of the P.C.C. I don't know who else they told, of course."

"What's P.C.C. mean?" asked Springer, frowning at his notebook.

"Parochial Church Council. We had an extraordinary meeting a few days ago, to confirm the arrangements for keeping watch in the church. Farrow was shouting about it then: the Vicar was keen, but I'm afraid the poor old chap was too easily persuaded by people like Farrow and Blanch."

"And if the gun was in fact in the vestry, who could have got access to it?"

"Anyone at all, I suppose. The vestry isn't locked when the church is open. The plate is kept in one safe, and the collection-money in another until it's been banked. There's nothing else of value, but anyone could go in if he chose a time when neither of the priests was using it."

"Strewth!" said Springer, unable to contain himself any longer.

Montero hurried him away, after getting Sarah White's address, and they made their way to the church. As Overley had said, nothing was locked up. Their feet rang sharply on the tiled floor as they strode, with more urgency than reverence, down the centre aisle and round to the side of the chancel. A watery sun peered through the dark stained glass and cast patterns more beautiful than the designs of the windows themselves, but the detectives were unaware of them. They entered the vestry and began carefully but rapidly to search, until Springer gave a yelp of discovery. A heavy old oak desk took up a large part of the wall opposite the door from the church and at an angle to the door which led outside. In one of its drawers, lying neatly on a pile of receipted bills, was a bright and well-oiled service revolver of an old type. Springer picked it up in a handkerchief, sniffed the barrel and clicked open the magazine.

"One shot missing, and it's been fired recently and not cleaned," he reported. "I think we'll be seeing that there Farrow again, sir."

However, Montero did not seem to be in a great hurry to see Farrow. Sarah White was not in the house where she lodged, a matter of no surprise since she had her living to earn as a teacher. They found the school a few streets away and youthful eyes peered through a dozen windows at this welcome break in the day's routine. In a room that smelt of chalk, disinfectant and strong tea, where unmarked papers lay in small, rebuking piles, they broke the news once again.

Sarah White was distressed but less ostentatiously than Overley had been. Like everyone else, she could think of no one who had the least reason to harm the Vicar. Certainly, some had done their best to make his life a misery.

"There's Miss Mason, for one. It used to sicken me how she would get up and denounce him at the least excuse. She seems to come to church only to make mischief."

"Do you mean that she disapproved of his level of churchmanship?" Montero asked mildly, beginning to feel lost in the midst of ecclesiastical subtlety.

"She's a black Prot," Miss White replied with fervour and acerbity.

"Still, we don't carry religious extremism to the extent of killing, nowadays, do we?" Montero said as gently as he could.

"I really couldn't say, but you'd better ask her yourself. She lives near to the church and she's always fussing about there."

"Really? Was she there when you went in yesterday evening?"

"How did you know that?" Fear glinted in Miss White's eyes; a safe, claw-stretching tabby became a desperate alley stray.

"Somebody mentioned it. Nothing wrong, surely?" Montero's eyes were so blue that he might have been looking on the world for the first time.

"No. No, of course not. I went into the church for a few minutes of private prayer. Oh! It can't have been long before the poor Vicar was killed."

"Did you see him in the church?"

"Yes, he was waiting to hear someone's confession. Do you think whoever it was could have been the murderer?"

Montero refused to be drawn, and they were soon leaving the school, aware still of countless eyes distracted from blackboards.

Miss Mason was at home, since she supported herself mainly by doing the more leisurely jobs of typing sent out by an agency. From her window the bulk of the church swelled above the intervening row of houses.

"A very convenient situation for a regular church-goer," Montero said.

"I'd rather the church were at the other end of the parish if it were more truly a house of God," Miss Mason replied. "But the parochial system is the heart of true English religion. All this chopping and changing is contrary to the Bible, and special chaplains are the work of Rome. If we don't all stick to our parishes, the next thing will be wandering friars selling relics and indulgences."

"Yes, I see. Well, Miss Mason, I don't know whether you can help us. You know – or perhaps you don't – about the Vicar —"

"Mrs. Acres rang up to tell me this morning. Well, he has gone to judgement where all his tricks and his crosses won't help him. Let us hope that he may somehow be saved."

"Quite. Now, we've just been having a talk with Miss White —"

"That woman is a daughter of Babylon." Miss Mason's mouth snapped open and shut; burning faggots seemed to threaten them all.

"Is she? I mean, she seems to have been one of the last to see the Vicar alive. I wondered whether you by any chance were in the church after about seven o'clock yesterday evening."

"At seven I was engaged on more godly work – preparing a beverage for one who follows the light of Truth without folly or fear."

Montero has the name of being one of the most adaptable and unshakeable members of the C.I.D. but he was beginning to have enough of Miss Mason's scale of values. Having found that she had nothing useful to tell them, except a long recital of the iniquities of the late Vicar and his followers, he hastily took his leave.

Springer by this time was muttering under his breath and looking almost demented.

"Stone the crows," he ejaculated when they had gained the sanctuary of their own car, "this is about the craziest case I've ever had to handle. You can't get a straight answer out of any of them."

"On the contrary, we've learned quite a lot, and I think there's more being hidden that won't be too hard to find. We'll go back to the Vicarage and have a proper conference."

They drove in silence through the streets that were full of morning activity. This corner of London carried a new death, the latest in centuries of mortality, and was outwardly unaffected by the fact of its violence and apparent lack of purpose. Yet somewhere, perhaps miles away by now or perhaps waiting to cross when their car passed the next corner, was the person who had coldly planned and carried out murder. The Vicarage was cold, its grates unswept while Mrs. Acres was busy telephoning around the parish. The two men kept on their coats and drew up a small table in the front room. In spite of everything, Montero seemed cheerful.

"Now, let's get things in order," he said. "As for motive, there seems to be none at all, so we've got to keep digging. When we know what was in the old man's will, we may be wiser. Means – lying in the vestry for anyone to pick up. The opportunities seem to be pretty open, since the Vicar would open the door to anyone.

All right, Jack, who's number one so far as you're concerned?"

"Farrow," Springer said emphatically. "Owns the gun, comes round here and uses it, slips out the back and runs into the young Curate. That's his bad luck, otherwise no one need have known he was here. He got in a mess about whether or not he went to the front door first. Now he's the treasurer of the whole works, so when he knows that the Vicar's got money to leave them, he decides to speed it up and get them out of debt."

"Why does he draw attention to the gun in the first place?" Montero asked.

"Double bluff, sir."

"Secondly, we don't know for certain whether or not his gun killed the Vicar, though we soon shall. Thirdly even the most devoted treasurer doesn't kill to augment funds for other people. All right, Jack, don't look so disconsolate. I'm just acting as *advocatus diaboli.*"

"Pardon, sir?" Springer said doubtfully.

"I'm helping our thought by putting the arguments on the other side. All this ecclesiastical conversation is affecting my vocabulary. I agree that Farrow is our most likely man, but let's go on. What about Malving?"

"But he's a parson, sir."

"Nevertheless – he was in and out of the vestry and could have got the gun any time. He has half an hour that he can't account for, hanging around the Vicarage on business that he won't divulge. Also, we know that he's disgruntled about not being allowed to get a proper house in time for his marriage, and that it was the Vicar who gave the casting vote which decided it. Not much of a motive, but worth remembering. What about the two churchwardens?"

"Well, either of them could have got the gun easy enough. Overley was in the church yesterday evening. He says he went back home, but what was to stop him following the Vicar and doing him in? Blanch seems to have a nice little alibi for himself, by being with our old pal Mr. Ludlow, but I think we ought to check times carefully. Neither of them has any sort of motive."

"Overley knows the value of old books," Montero said.

Springer thought this over and nodded agreement.

"It's a proper lark to have Ludlow popping up," he said. "If we don't get a move on, he'll be solving the case for us again."

"Not this time," Montero said grimly.

"Well, that seems to be the lot, unless we turn up anybody else with a grudge against the old man," Springer said.

"Except for Mr. X," said Montero.

"Who's he?"

"Let's call him the Unknown Penitent. The Vicar was in church, waiting to hear a confession outside his regular times. Suppose whoever it was came back to the Vicarage with him, perhaps for more help outside the formal confession? Or suppose that person never turned up at the church, and was waiting for him when he came back? There's somebody who was one of the last to see him alive, and who knew just what his movements would be around the time when the killing took place. Guilty or not, that person can help us with our inquiries, as the papers always put it so delicately."

"We seem to be scrambling, sir," Springer said.

"I don't think so entirely. The Vicar was seen in church soon after seven, and the doctor's sure he was killed by half past, so that narrows things quite a bit. He could hardly have been back here, put his car in the garage and got into his study before seven-fifteen at the earliest. It's rather more than five minutes' drive, and it was neither the sort of car nor driver to move very fast. We've got the time within fifteen minutes, and if he hears this confession or waited for much longer, it must have been even closer to seven-thirty. This seems to let out Malving, but we'll have to check his times. Now that brings us to something interesting."

"Malving locked the church," Springer said.

"Just so. If he locked up between seven-thirty and eight and was pottering about there all that time, the murderer didn't have much chance of returning the gun to the vestry. Yet it was there this morning. Therefore someone took a colossal risk early this morning, or it was done by one of the people with a key to the church."

"Weren't they going to keep a watch there?" Springer asked.

"It seems that they have been doing so. And last night the task fell on – Cyril Blanch. We'd better find out whether he fulfilled it."

"Why bother to return the gun at all? I mean, with so many people getting at it, who would worry whether it was found? I don't see it, sir!"

"Neither do I. Taking it away was fairly easy, but it was asking for trouble to take it back after the murder had been discovered. Odd."

"Shall we have another look at the diary?" Springer suggested, seeing the chief suddenly downcast.

Together they studied the diary which had lain open on the Vicar's desk. The previous day seemed to have been uneventful until its terrible ending. The only entries were:

8.0 Early Mass. N.B. Intercession for missions
12.30 Lunch – Mothers' Union Committee
Mrs. Acres out from 5.30. Supper in oven

Then came the last, almost illegible scrawl: *Re July 23.*

"He was trying to leave some kind of message just before he died," Montero said. "We'd better see what he was doing on the twenty-third of July. Presumably it was this year he meant – let's try, anyway."

He turned back the pages, with their records of ministration to so many aspects of life and death. The entry for the twenty-third of July, in the Vicar's shaky but neat handwriting, read as follows:

> *Malving goes on holiday*
> *10.30 Farrow*
> *4.15 Scouts' prizes*
> *N.B. Tell Mrs. Acres about Sarah White*

"Now who was he pointing to there?" Montero wondered. "Four people mentioned, including the one we're particularly interested in at the moment. And what on earth was he to tell Mrs. Acres about Sarah White. We'd better try to straighten out those entries as soon as we can."

While Montero and Springer were interviewing possible witnesses, Ludlow was sitting comfortably in his room in college. It was a busy morning, at a stage in the first term of the academic year when the students are just beginning to divide themselves neatly into potential sheep and goats. On this occasion it was the goats who were most in evidence, and Ludlow's patience was wearing thin by the time he had a few minutes to himself. With the air of a man undertaking a great task he reached for the first of the essays waiting to be marked. After correcting two spelling mistakes in the title he put it down again and sighed deeply.

Ludlow's next actions would have puzzled any of his colleagues who could have seen them. After making quite sure that his door was firmly closed, he drew the curtains over the narrow window which offered the view of an unprepossessing courtyard. Then he dived into the inner pocket of his bulging jacket, pulled out a handful of papers and selected one which he unfolded, laid on the desk, and studied intently with his head in his hands. His illicit minutes with the Vicar's diary on the previous evening had not been wasted and he had made a transcript of some of the entries. What now occupied his attention had been written a few days before the diary came to its abrupt and cryptic end. In the middle of the usual record of appointments, the Vicar had written:

Books delivered. N.B. must make safe; perhaps IK69
    A Garland of Spiritual Delights, 1869
    Of the Invocation of Airy and Earthy Spirits n.d.
    Sermons of the Reverend Ezekiel Banter, 1734
    The Spanish Tragedy, 1592
    Collected Poems of William Wordsworth, 1900
    The Small House at Allington, 1897

Ludlow read and re-read the list of titles, and shook his head like a man who cannot believe what he sees. He got up and went to his shelves and spent some time with a thick volume of reference. Then he gave a long, low whistle, picked up the sheet of paper and very carefully folded it into the safest part of his wallet.

CHAPTER SIX

Ludlow's colleagues would agree that he possesses at least one characteristic to a high degree, though they might disagree about the name of it: his friends would say that he has an inquiring mind, his enemies that he is excessively inquisitive. It is a characteristic which has brought him into some strange places and some unlikely company, and it was being exercised strongly after his journey with Blanch to the Vicarage. The list of books and the accompanying mysterious reference which he had copied from the Vicar's diary took up a good deal of his spare time. Whenever he was alone, he was likely to unfold his precious sheet of paper and study it with a mixture of surprise, incredulity and bewilderment. In spite of his previous encounters with crime, that little piece of paper seemed to interest him far more than the fact that there had been a murder.

At least, it was so until Cyril Blanch came to see him. There was a hesitant knock on Ludlow's door, and the invitation to come in admitted not a shy student but a crestfallen colleague. Without being particularly arrogant or extrovert, Blanch usually seemed to convey the fact that he held a fairly good opinion of his own character and ability. On this occasion, however, he looked as if he wanted to crawl under the desk and not be noticed. He also looked as if he had not slept recently.

"How nice to see you," Ludlow said without great conviction. "Do sit down, if you can find a clear space anywhere."

Blanch sat and stared at the floor, while Ludlow regarded him with his usual shrewd benevolence.

"I'm terribly worried," Blanch murmured.

"Dear me, I'm sorry to hear that. I hope there hasn't been any more trouble in your church. Those unfortunate attacks put one in mind of the strange mixture of fascination and repulsion which was so often engendered in past writers by black magic and witchcraft. You will of course recall how Shakespeare —'

"No, not that," Blanch interrupted desperately. "The fact is – look, do you remember what time I arrived at your place the other evening?"

"At precisely quarter to eight. You were fifteen minutes late, a matter of no importance in the circumstances, but I am somewhat sensitive to the passage of time when I am waiting without any particular occupation."

"Yes. Well, I wondered – you know the policeman who seems to be investigating the murder of the Vicar, don't you?"

"Inspector Montero and I have spent some interesting times together. He is a remarkably intelligent man, well-read and not addicted to the modern cult of all things scientific. You wouldn't get on with him at all," Ludlow added maliciously.

"I'm not prepared to accept that pure mathematics is simply a science," Blanch said with some indignation. "If you were capable of understanding them, I could present you with some concepts of philosophical significance —"

"But to return to the point," said Ludlow, impatient of any digressions except his own, "what has all this to do with my acquaintance with Inspector Montero and his good sergeant?"

"Presumably your word would carry some weight with him. He may come asking you what time I arrived, so perhaps you wouldn't mind saying it was a bit earlier. I mean, say I got to you just before half past seven."

"Why should I say that?" Ludlow asked, all innocence.

"They've been after me, asking questions about what I was doing that evening. I hadn't any particular proof of the time before you saw me. I was just reading quietly until I left to drive over to you, but that doesn't seem to satisfy them. And they wanted to know whether I went to the church later that night, to keep my turn there."

"And did you?"

"Yes, and that seems to make them suspicious too. They asked me a lot of questions about how I got on with the Vicar and how much I knew about his will. And they wanted to know if I'd seen the books he bought recently. Of course I hadn't. I leave that sort of thing to Overley."

"You don't like Overley," Ludlow murmured to the ceiling.

"You've no right to say that – you're as bad as they are, twisting every word I say." Blanch jumped up and then sat down again sheepishly. "I'm sorry, Ludlow, it's not like me to get out of control. This affair is worrying me a lot, so if you can see your way to stretching the time by about twenty minutes, it might satisfy them."

"I couldn't possibly tell a lie to provide you with an alibi." Ludlow looked his most priggish, and it is something he can do outstandingly well even against the heavy competition of his colleagues. Then his reasonable compassion reasserted itself.

"I don't think you're the sort of man to commit a murder, and I'm prepared to say that to Montero," he said gently. "If I can discover or think of anything that might point to the real murderer, I shall make full use of it, whoever may be involved. Does that help you?"

"I suppose so." Blanch seemed hardly to care any more.

"Perhaps I could have a look round this afternoon, provided I can get these essays marked in time."

Blanch took the hint and went, leaving Ludlow looking very thoughtful. After a few minutes the essays were still unmarked but the mysterious piece of paper was being studied yet again. That afternoon was a Wednesday and free from lectures. As Ludlow made his way out of the main gates of the college, two coaches were filling up with hearty young men and women on their way to play games. Ludlow shuddered at the thought and looked distastefully at the equipment prepared for so much energy. With carefully measured steps, and trying to listen to his own heartbeats, he started on his journey.

The church was open as usual but seemed to be empty. Ludlow went in and stood for a time studying the scene as if preparing to write a critical essay about it. He sniffed, whether with approval or distaste, at the lingering smell of incense. At the far end was the simple confessional, the chair for the priest and the kneeling-desk with a crucifix above it for the penitent. It looked peaceful, not the witness of a man's last few minutes of life. In one or two places the walls showed lighter patches, where offending words and drawings had been scrubbed off after the recent attacks. The stained-glass windows were mercifully almost opaque against the grey November afternoon.

"Hullo, do come along and have a proper look round."

Malving, tall and confident in his neat cassock with a narrow leather belt, was at his elbow, emerged from some secret place before Ludlow could see him coming.

"I rather think we've met before," Malving went on cheerfully.

"We saw each other at the Vicarage. Not under conditions that would make for willing recognition."

"Oh yes, you came in with Cyril Blanch. I remember now. That awful evening doesn't bear much thinking about, does it? Did you know the Vicar at all?"

"I never met him, and on that occasion I arrived a few

minutes too late. A pity, because I think we should have had some interests in common.''

"He was a fine man, and a wonderful priest. I still can't get used to the idea that I shan't be able to ask his advice on anything again. He never seemed to get discouraged by anything. You know, it isn't always easy to keep on and on trying in a parish like this.''

Malving suddenly looked young and tired and vulnerable. Ludlow found himself liking him and wishing he could help, but he had come there for a purpose that he was determined to follow.

"When did you last see him?'' he asked.

"Earlier in the day when it happened, just briefly. I didn't think it was going to be the last time. I must have just missed him here in the evening, because several people saw him sitting at the confessional around seven o'clock. I was here about half past, but he'd gone by then.''

"You expected to find him at home soon after that,'' Ludlow said.

"Well, it was a fair chance, and I particularly wanted a private chat with him. I didn't know then that he'd been here so soon before me. It wasn't one of his regular times for confession.''

"Would he have come at an irregular time?'' Ludlow asked.

"Oh yes, either of us would always be ready to hear a confession by special appointment if the circumstances required it.''

"What sort of circumstances?"

"Well, if a person had something particularly worrying, and couldn't ever get along at one of the ordinary times. Or if someone had to go away suddenly on a journey, or was going into danger. And a first confession is usually a pretty lengthy affair and needs a time to itself."

"I see." Ludlow looked thoughtful and interested. "Have you any idea for whom he might have been waiting at that time?"

"None at all. Anyway, it's not the sort of thing that one would discuss, even with another priest."

Malving clearly did not want to say any more on the subject. Ludlow did not press it, but allowed himself to be shown some of the few features of note which the church possessed. Eventually the priest took his leave, and Ludlow was left to his own devices. The church had not in fact been completely deserted when he came in, for his arrival and his encounter with Malving had been watched by a man who appeared to be fast asleep in the corner of a back pew. A casual observer would have said that he was an old man, but his eyes were alert when he opened them wide and his skin was not very wrinkled under his load of dirt and hair. He was wearing a decrepit overcoat with a piece of rope supplying the lack of buttons. Ludlow went and sat near him, without seeming to take any notice.

"Questions and no answers, questions and no answers. They're all the same, all in a gang together," Ludlow said in a depressed monotone which would have set his colleagues in the department of psychology twittering. His stratagem was effective, however; aroused by the call of another paranoiac, the man slid along towards him and arrived in a wave of methylated spirit.

"Take courage, my friend, they won't have it their own way for ever," he said. His voice was surprisingly gentle and not without education. His wild, bloodshot eyes were more sad than fierce.

"What happened to the old Vicar, then?" Ludlow asked.

"They did for him. One of them did for him. He was a decent old chap, not one of *them*. He had a good word for me, not like some who crawl on their knees and spit in your face. I've seen plenty, sitting here when they think I'm asleep."

"He was here that night when they came to get him," Ludlow said.

"So he was, so he was – sitting over there where they go to tell their secrets. And it wasn't a regular time for him to be there either."

"You're sure it was the Vicar?"

"Course I'm sure. Haven't I seen him over there enough times, with his white shirt and his little round hat?"

"Biretta. Was there anything about his behaviour to excite remark on that occasion?" Ludlow asked, forgetting his role.

"Eh?" The shabby man looked suspicious.

"Did he look as if he knew they were coming to get him?"

"Not he, poor old chap. There he sat, waiting and waiting for the one who never came. Then he got up and went off to the vestry over there, taking off that green thing round his neck and folding it as if he were a bit sad about something."

"Stole." Ludlow said, automatically supplying information.

"Never stole it, not him. Who are you, making charges like the rest of them? You came here to get me, did you?"

"No, no. That thing he wears round his neck like a scarf is called a stole. Never mind. Now look, was it definitely not the other priest, the young Curate?"

"What, Mr. Malving? Look, you've seen him, mate. He's about twice the height the old man was and could give him three times round the shoulders. He came in later, after they'd all gone. Stood mucking about for a bit, in and out the vestry, then he came and chucked me out and locked the door on me. He gave me a bob, though."

"Who else was here then, while the Vicar was at the confessional?"

"That Overley came and went – he's sly, for all his piety and his bowing and scraping and bobbing up and down. And Sarah White, looking like her own name. There's something worrying her all right. Maybe they're after her too."

"You seem to know them all," Ludlow remarked.

"I see them, oh yes, I see them. And the other one, who came in after the Vicar went, but he was new. Dressed all in black but not a parson. He walked about peering at things and making noises as if he was going to be sick. We get them sometimes, friends of that Miss Mason, I reckon."

"Well, thank you for your help," Ludlow said with a polite return to normality. "Perhaps we shall be able to talk again."

"Don't tell *them*. They'll come for me if they know I've been talking. They send messages, you know, waves through the air to read your thoughts. They know what you're doing, all the time, and they hate us, they want to finish us off."

He started to babble incoherently; Ludlow disentangled himself and went out of the church feeling mingled compassion and incompetence. There was little satisfaction in dredging information out of holes that the Welfare State had not yet been able to fill. He made his way through a warren of streets to the Vicarage, where his previous arrival with Cyril Blanch and his acquaintance with Montero proved to be credentials enough. After the first shock, Mrs. Acres was enjoying being a centre of interest and seemed to regret only that she had no more information to give. Ludlow flattered her for a time and then expressed a wish to see the books that the Vicar had recently bought.

"Well you may ask," Mrs. Acres said. "First the

police, then Mr. Overley and now you – and me not able to give a straight answer to any of you. The plain fact is, sir, that I don't know what the poor man did with them and I doubt whether he knew himself. One day he had them there in his study, going through them and him all lost to the world as he was whenever he had a book in his hand. Next day they might have been taken off by an angel to the moon for all anyone could see of them."

"It would seem then that he deposited them somewhere known only to himself," Ludlow said, sorting out this mixture as well as he could. "I understand that it was his habit to do that and then make a note to remind himself."

Mrs. Acres agreed that it was, but gave it as her opinion that his reminders were no use to anyone else and little even to himself.

"His mind worked in a funny sort of way," she explained. "There was nothing wrong with him, you understand, but he liked to put things all twisted and difficult. Did you ever try one of those crossword puzzles, sir?"

"Indeed yes, a pleasant enough relaxation. One prefers those which demand knowledge as well as ingenuity and do not depend on a mere proliferation of anagrams."

"Ah. Well, the Vicar was a proper one for them, and he used to think that kind of way sometimes, if you take my meaning."

"Yes, I think I do. It will be a nuisance if the books

don't turn up before the estate has to be settled. No doubt his family will be anxious to have them found – I believe there is a nephew, isn't there?"

"There certainly is, more's the pity. The dear man had no family left that you could call a family, only this one fellow who looks to be no good to anyone."

"You've seen him, then?"

"He was round here not more than a week or two ago, as bold as brass after never coming near the place before that I know of. I didn't like the look of him when I let him in, for all he was related to the good old man. But like doesn't always mate with like, to my way of thinking. Sure enough, it wasn't long before there were high words between them."

"The Vicar and his nephew had a quarrel?"

"Well now, the Vicar wouldn't have quarrelled with anyone. But this fellow was shouting and after a bit he came out as black as thunder and pushed past me as if I wasn't there – I'd just happened to be passing the door of the study, you understand, not that I was interested in what they were up to. He went out all in a rage, but he didn't know what I heard before he went. I didn't say a word to the Vicar, not wanting to worry him, but now perhaps it would have been better if I had."

"What did he say?" Ludlow asked with excitement.

"I wouldn't repeat the words to a gentleman, but he was making all sorts of threats. He looked as if he could kill anyone who got in his way. Oh dear, it's made me come over all faint to think of it. Won't you let me make a cup of tea, Mr. Ludlow? And you look as if you'd be none the worse for one or two of my rock cakes, if you'll forgive me saying so."

She looked with meaningful regard at Ludlow's thin frame. Ludlow dislikes tea and cakes about equally, but he is prepared to sacrifice himself to the pursuit of knowledge. With a concealed sigh, he followed Mrs. Acres down to the basement.

While Ludlow was passing a sociable hour with Mrs. Acres, Benjamin Farrow was having a much less pleasant time in his own home. While his wife hovered and sniffed in the passage outside, he sat at bay in the drawing-room crammed with old weapons, military pictures and trophies of his own and others' wars. Montero sat opposite him, occasionally getting up and walking about to throw his questions from different directions, while Springer on an upright chair looked like a hound about to pounce on its prey. Those who knew Montero only in his gentle, urbane mood would have found it hard to recognise him.

"When you left here that evening," Montero said, "you didn't go straight to the Vicarage as you have stated. You went first to the church, to which you have a key and which by that time had been shut for the night. You took your gun from the vestry, went to the Vicarage and were admitted by the back way after you had tapped on the study window. There was a quarrel, provoked deliberately by you, in the course of which you drew your gun and shot the Vicar. You were making your escape when you saw Malving at the front door and were obliged to stop and talk to him to avoid suspicion. Later that night, or early next morning, you went back to the church and replaced your gun.''

Even as he spoke, he could feel the weaknesses in his accusation and the impossibility of proving it without further evidence. Driven into a corner, Farrow blustered and threatened proceedings for defamation.

''I shall get a solicitor,'' he shouted.

''That would be a very good idea,'' Montero said, ''and you'd better get a good one. We have proof that it was your gun which killed the Vicar. The best thing you can do is make a complete statement.''

''I have nothing more to say,'' Farrow muttered. ''My wife knows that I didn't leave the house until a few minutes before I arrived at the Vicarage that evening.''

''Nobody knows what time you did arrive there. If you went to the front door first, why didn't you meet Mr. Malving?''

''I don't know. Well – look here – I actually went straight to the back. I wanted a private word with the Vicar and I didn't know then that Mrs. Acres was out. That's the only thing that wasn't absolutely true in what I've told you.''

''Why were you afraid of being seen by Mrs. Acres?''

''It wasn't a question of being afraid. She's a notorious gossip, and there was no need to have every movement spread all over the parish. My business with the Vicar was confidential.''

"What was it, Mr. Farrow?"

"It was to do with the parish accounts. I'm saying no more, and you can't make me."

"Quite true, sir." Montero yawned as if bored with the conversation then suddenly swung round with his eyes as hard as steel. "You've admitted to having no licence for the gun, and that's a criminal offence. Further, you've been guilty of extreme negligence in leaving a loaded gun where anyone could take it. We shall be talking to you again – many more times. I've more than enough to arrest you now. You're to report to your local police station every day, and if you miss just once I shall put you where you'll stay."

"I reckon he did it all right, sir," Springer said when they had taken their leave of Farrow and his tearful wife, "but we're going to have a hell of a job proving it."

"I know, Jack." Montero pulled his little moustache as he did when he was perplexed. "For one thing, there seems to be no possible motive. Then there were so many people who could have got at the gun even when the church was locked, let alone any other time in the day. Why did he make such a show of the thing if he was going to use it?"

"Just so that a lot of people *could* have used it instead," Springer suggested.

"That may well be, but a good lawyer would make a defence out of it in court. Just run through the list of those who had a key to the church again."

"The Vicar – he's dead and his keys weren't missing. Malving, the Curate. Farrow, Overley, Blanch. Also the verger and the organist, who don't seem to come into the picture and anyway have good alibis for the whole time. There's the possibility that a copy was made at some time, of course."

"There's also the possibility that the gun was taken during the day when the church was open and deserted. But how was it put back? Malving was in the church about the time the Vicar was killed and stayed there until he locked up. Blanch spent the night there until Malving came in for the early service. So either someone with a key slipped back before Blanch came, or someone else took a colossal risk during a short period next morning."

"Or else either Blanch or Malving did it, sir."

"Yes, but Malving is pretty well covered by the time we've checked that he spent at the hospital. It's hardly possible, unless his scooter moves at supersonic speed. Blanch would have had to move fast too, but it's possible."

"I wouldn't trust Mr. Ludlow to know the time ten minutes either way, from what I've seen of him," Springer said.

"He's conscious enough of time when he chooses – such as when someone keeps him waiting. I think we can be pretty sure that Blanch was with him by quarter to eight."

They drove in silence until they were nearly back at

Scotland Yard. The evening traffic was beginning to pile up in the dusk, pouring its urgent, noisy stream across Waterloo Bridge. They waited at the lights, neither of them in the mood for the joking exchanges which they often shared.

"What about that nephew as Mrs. Acres was so down on?" Springer asked. "If he comes in for a good share out of the will, he had a lovely motive. I'd like to ask him a few questions."

"So would I, if we could find him. There's really no justification for putting out that he's officially wanted, but maybe we ought to do it. I hope he'll turn up soon."

CHAPTER SEVEN

Ludlow collected his notes, looked in vain for the paper-clip which had held them together and was now attached in forgetfulness to his lapel, and went out of the lecture-room. The students thrust their own papers into folders and came after him. A small, brown man from one of the countries that no longer fly the British flag and send their youth to Britain with happier faces, trotted resolutely until he had caught up with Ludlow.

"Sir, I am wanting to ask you some questions," he announced.

Ludlow never minds giving extra time to students and has a particularly soft spot for those from overseas. The fact that his reaction was slower and less enthusiastic than usual may perhaps be traced to the copy from the Vicar's diary which still reposed in his pocket and was beginning to get very battered with constant examination.

"You are saying how Shakespeare's choruses make direct appeal to audience as well as commenting on play. Can you please give example for my essay?"

"You should find your own examples," Ludlow said kindly. "Test all assertions against your reading and either confirm or reject them by what you find. However, let us take one instance to start you off. You are, I trust, familiar with *Henry V*."

"Oh yes, my teacher at home says it is a play of British Imperialism."

"Does he, indeed? Well, be that as it may, let us consider the effect on a London audience little more than a decade after the Armada when the chorus comes out and tells them that

> Now all the youth of England is on fire
> And silken dalliance in the wardrobe lies,
> Now thrive, the armourers, and honour's thought
> Sits solely in the breast of every man —"

Ludlow was working himself to a fine histrionic declamation as he came into his own corridor. A man who appeared to be writing something on the door of his room fell back with startled amazement. Still clutching the piece of paper which he had been resting on the door for support, he stood with open mouth as Ludlow and the student advanced. He was apparently in his early forties, wearing a waist-length motoring coat with a leather collar turned up to his rather prominent ears. His fair hair stuck up in irregular spikes at the back but had already receded from his forehead. His face was unhealthily sallow, his eyes large, blue and cheeky.

Finishing his recitation neatly at the door, Ludlow

walked into his office with the student on his heels and made straight for his bookcase. Turning with a book already open for reference, he was annoyed and surprised to see that the sallow man had also come in and was standing with his hands in his pockets as if he meant to make himself at home there. Ludlow glared at him and spoke to the student.

"I'm glad to have caught you after all," the sallow man said.

"Not now, not now," Ludlow replied testily. "Come back after lunch."

"Professor Ludlow, it's very important for me to talk to you."

Now Ludlow is as open to flattery by suggestion as most men, and even though he knows that the title of professor is tossed about with less discrimination outside the universities than it is inside, there is something pleasant in the sound. He now dismissed the student with a few notes of things to read, then sat down behind the desk and gestured his visitor to a chair. The sallow man lit a cigarette and held it in stained fingers.

"I hear that you're interested in old books," he said. His voice was more pleasant than his manner.

"In some old books," Ludlow said cautiously. "Age alone is not always a recommendation."

"What about these?" The other fished out three or four books from inside his coat and handed them to Ludlow who gave them a quick examination.

"These are of no value," Ludlow said. "They're cheap

late-Victorian editions of popular novels. You can get them in any secondhand shop."

"Not old enough for you, eh?" Seeming not in the least put out, but rather pleased with Ludlow's answer, the sallow man took back his books.

"Neither old enough nor rare enough. I'm sorry to disappoint you, but if you've no further questions —"

"Something Elizabethan would be worth more, I suppose?"

"Well, any book printed in the Elizabethan period is rare enough to be interesting, and some are almost priceless. But you won't pick up a First Folio of Shakespeare nowadays."

"Might pick up something by Kyd, though." Ludlow's acquaintances would have been surprised to see the effect on him of those casual words. He nearly leapt out of his chair and his mouth opened wordlessly.

"I won't take up any more of your time, then. It's a good thing I saw you – I was just writing a note asking to see you when you came along. Let me know if you pick up any of those Elizabethan bargains, and I'll do the same for you – be seeing you."

Ludlow carried this strange interview with him all day and was still trying to work it out when he got back to his flat in the evening. He was in the kitchen, producing clouds of blue smoke and refreshing himself from time to time from a bottle of dry sherry, when the doorbell rang imperiously. Muttering maledictions, and wiping his hands on anything within reach, Ludlow went and opened the door to reveal Montero standing outside.

"Good God, are you on fire?" were Montero's first words.

"I am cooking a curry," Ludlow said with dignity. "Come in and pour yourself a drink if you can find a glass. I must attend to my poppadums. Perhaps you'll join me when I've finished the preparation."

"It will have to taste better than it looks." Montero peered dubiously into the bubbling saucepans.

"Of course it will – good food always does," Ludlow said. "You can usually distrust food that looks like a picture in a magazine, because it may well taste like one. Did you come here simply to criticise my cooking?"

"I came to look up an old friend, prompted by our unexpected meeting the other evening." Montero perched himself on a stool in the kitchen and started eating mango chutney with a spoon.

"Don't do that," Ludlow said severely. "If you want to make yourself useful you can try to find where I put the strainer for the rice. I suppose the truth is that you need my help."

"I wouldn't think of troubling you with my problems. Since you show so much interest in them, however, may I ask whether you discussed them with your visitor this morning?" Montero smiled pleasantly and seemed hardly interested in Ludlow's reaction, but his eyes missed nothing.

"I don't know what you mean." Ludlow burnt his finger and swore.

"Come now, we don't try to fool each other any longer, do we? You had a visitor at noon today, and he talked about the murder of the Vicar. I can't put it any plainer than that for you."

"I certainly had an unexpected caller," Ludlow said, "and I've yet to learn that this is any crime. We talked about neither vicars nor murder."

"What did you talk about, then?"

"Old books."

"It might come to the same thing, mightn't it?"

"Your logic is on a different plane from mine, Inspector."

The two men looked at each other, sparring with a mutual respect and some affection, trying not to cough in the billowing smoke from the stove.

"Come on," Montero said, "who was he?"

"I honestly don't know. He gave no name. Do you know who he is?"

"No, but I know that he called at the Vicarage this morning, had a long conversation with Mrs. Acres and made straight for your college when he came out."

"You're up to your old tricks," Ludlow said admonishingly, "putting policemen to follow people without proof."

"We happen to be interested in anyone who calls at the Vicarage just at present. It will delight your wicked heart to know that our man lost him in the tube soon after he left you, and that he looked very much as if he knew that he was being followed. His whole behaviour was very suspicious."

"You've got a suspicious mind, anyway," Ludlow said. "Give me that spoon – no, the wooden one. If I knew I was being followed I should do just the same."

Montero unwisely took a deep breath and coughed. Ludlow handed him a glass of water, firmly corked the sherry bottle and went on stirring.

"Look here," Montero said when speech was restored to him, "I've good reason to respect your skill in solving matters that don't concern you. In my time in the Force I've learned when to stick to the book and when to play it by ear. Come clean with me, and I'll put you in the picture as well, because I think I can trust you. Now tell me who the man was; it may be important."

"I honestly don't know. I certainly hadn't seen him before. He brought some books for my opinion but they were quite worthless."

"Did you talk about the Vicar at all, or his diary?"

"Not a word."

"Now look, I know that you concealed a large sheet of paper when I chased you out of the Vicar's study, and I'll bet my pension that you'd been copying down bits. Maybe I ought to do something about it, but I won't so long as you don't trespass too far. Have you any idea where those books are?"

"Not even the beginning of an idea."

"All right, I believe you. And now I'll give you a few

bits of information and see what you make of them."
Ludlow opened the sherry bottle again and pushed it
towards Montero. "We've been looking at the Vicar's
will, which was with his solicitor. Thank goodness he
hadn't mislaid *that*, anyway. As we'd expected, there
was quite a lot of money – he'd inherited a considerable
private fortune and he'd lived frugally. The nephew,
whose name is Tom Finchley by the way, gets five
thousand, plus half the profit from the sale of the old
man's books. Mrs. Acres gets a straight thousand and
another thousand goes to the Guild of Saints Cyprian
and Severus."

"What on earth is that?"

"A society which seems to approve of the late Vicar's
level of practice: we shall be calling on the secretary in
due course. By the way, one of the parishioners, a Miss
Mason, is furious about it and is trying to get the bequest
annulled or whatever the legal term may be. Apart
from a few small sums, the residue of the estate goes to
the parish."

"Including the other half of the sale of his books?"
Ludlow asked thoughtfully.

"Yes. Now do you see why I'm interested in people
who go round talking about old books?"

"Help me to put these things on the table," Ludlow
said.

They ate industriously and in silence until most of
the curry was gone. Ludlow wiped his mouth, took a
long drink and looked hard at his unexpected guest.

"Who is this nephew?" he asked.

"As far as we've been able to find out, it's a fairly simple story. The Vicar had a sister, younger than himself, who made a very unfortunate marriage. Apparently her husband was an utter waster who eventually went off and left her with a child – the nephew in question. The Vicar used to try to help her with money, but she'd never take anything and more or less cut herself off from all her old life and associates. I gather she took to drink or drugs in the end. Anyway, she and the husband are both dead and the Vicar decided to make some provision for the nephew. So if you meet anyone called Tom Finchley, let me know about it."

"Thank you," said Ludlow, looking less complacent than he had at the beginning of the conversation. "I wish I had something useful for you, but I haven't – unless I can tell you anything about the books."

"I thought you'd made a list. What's your opinion?"

"Most of them are worth little or nothing, being just reprints or works of no modern interest. However, one or two of them may be extremely important. For instance, I should say that one is some kind of *grimoire*."

Ludlow paused and looked at Montero in the hope of having caught him out in something at last. He was still to find that the inspector was a worthy intellectual adversary.

"A book of witchcraft rituals," Montero said. "Yes, and there've been outbreaks of what appears to be some kind of Satanism or Black Magic in the church. Those who take these things seriously would give a lot to get hold of a book like that."

"So I thought. Secondly, there's a copy of *The Spanish Tragedy*, which was written by Thomas Kyd—"

"And is one of the outstanding examples of the Elizabethan tragedy of revenge. An early copy would be pretty valuable."

"If the date in the Vicar's list is correct, this one would be beyond price."

"Explain," Montero said tersely.

"Briefly," said Ludlow, very pleased at knowing something more than Montero at last, "this particular edition was printed in contravention of the true copyright – admittedly a dubious business in the sixteenth century. The copies were confiscated, and so far only one has been known to exist: it's in the British Museum."

"So if the Vicar did chance to get hold of one in an odd bundle of books, both his nephew and the parish would be substantially better off. Not many people would know about the value, though."

"No, but anyone who had the details and was intelligent enough to use the right reference books could soon find out. An antiquarian bookseller would probably notice it at once."

"Overley denies having seen the books," Montero said. "Well, I must be on my way. Thanks for the curry – I'll reciprocate one day, if you haven't poisoned me. Meanwhile, be good."

Ludlow was kept busy on the following day, and it was late in the afternoon before he was able to satisfy his curiosity any further. He reached Overley's shop as the dusk was drawing to darkness, accompanied by a thin drizzle which made the pavements greasy. The blind was drawn down on the glass door, but there was a light inside and the door opened when Ludlow tentatively pushed it. Overley came out through a narrow gap between tightly-packed shelves and looked helpful.

"I haven't anything particularly in mind," Ludlow said, "but I'm most interested in books printed in the sixteenth century. I don't suppose you get much from that period, do you?"

"There's not a lot on the market," Overley admitted. "It's chiefly a question of looking out for auctions and having a bit of luck. I've one or two little things here that might interest you."

He produced some volumes which Ludlow examined critically and rejected.

"What I'm mainly interested in," he said, "are early editions of Elizabethan plays."

"That's a very difficult field for collections, I'm afraid. If you'd like to leave your name and address, I could certainly let you know if anything comes my way."

"No, it doesn't matter. Another subject that I'm interested in is witchcraft. Have you any old books on the raising of spirits and things like that?"

Overley went red and tightened his fists.

"I've nothing of that sort," he said. "People talk about being interested in it, without beginning to understand the real implications. I'd advise you not to meddle with things like that, if you value your soul. It's an evil thing, and I've seen the effects of it here in this very parish."

"Ah yes, I heard there'd been some unpleasant happenings. That reminds me – the late Vicar was a great lover of old books, wasn't he?"

"Yes, he was," said Overley, seeming to control his anger with an effort.

"He must have been a remarkable man."

"He was a saint."

"I wish I'd known him. Tell me, was he interested in codes and ciphers at all?"

"I couldn't say."

Overley turned away as if dismissing Ludlow, who did not take his leave but settled down to browsing among the shelves. A minute or two later, the doorbell jangled again and Farrow came in, carrying a walking-stick and looking very military. Ludlow faded even closer into the background of books and kept his ears alert. Unfortunately for him, Overley and Farrow spoke in whispers and obviously did not intend to share their business with anyone. They kept glancing at Ludlow and were looking by no means friendly; he decided that there was no more to be gained at present and that he might as well go.

"Just a minute, please."

As Ludlow turned towards the door, Farrow suddenly barred his way with an upraised stick. Ludlow looked down on the rotund, red-faced figure and was unsure whether it looked formidable or ridiculous. The whole scene was on the verge of melodrama.

"I know you," Farrow said accusingly. "You turned up at the Vicarage with Cyril Blanch, the night that the poor Vicar was killed."

"Well, what about it?" Ludlow asked.

"It was a very opportune moment to appear."

"I don't follow you."

"Blanch has a fine story of being in your company all the evening. How long did it take you to think up that?"

"This is a monstrous accusation," Ludlow said. "How dare you stand there and accuse me of conniving at perjury?"

"All right, tell me this – does Blanch deny being in the church earlier that day, and going back there in the night?"

"Not as far as I know. Why should he? I understood that this was part of an agreed plan."

"You mean that you had it all worked out between you?" Farrow asked with a leer.

Ludlow grasped the restraining stick and pushed it angrily aside. It was a long time since he had lost his temper and he had no wish to be drawn into the violence of which he had too often seen the consequences. But he was trembling as he walked out into the street, and he banged the door behind him with a force that made the glass rattle.

Was it anger for himself that tasted so bitterly in his mouth and made his heart beat faster, or was it recognition of a wrong done to the innocent and defenceless? Was Farrow's hostility the aggression of a trapped animal, or was it simple guilt? Certainly there were things to be learnt about oneself, when urbanity was stripped back and the naked encounter proved to be only hatred and fear. The pious words, the ordered routine of parish duties, could be weak shields in the face of real evil.

It was a fair test of a man's religion, and so far nobody seemed to be coming out of it very well. There might be many ways of seeing purpose and meaning when an old man bled to death over his own desk, but one way surely was to find the truth out of so many blunders and concealments. Ludlow was not feeling particularly proud of himself, but his mind was already clearer when he came to the end of the darkening street.

"I'm not a cipher expert, and I don't seem to be getting much help from those who claim to be."

It was a rare thing for Inspector Montero to blame anyone else for difficulties in a case he was handling, and the outburst showed that he was not at his best. It could have been the after-effects of Ludlow's curry, but

Springer seemed to be equally disconsolate as he stood in the office and nodded at his chief's words. The Vicar's diary lay open on the desk, its record of love and toil and human frailty now only an exhibit to be studied and used in evidence.

"Let's check everything again," Montero said without enthusiasm. "Malving went off for his summer holiday on the twenty-third of July, as the diary said. It had been arranged long before, and there seems to be no particular reason for using that day as a pointer to him. Farrow came to see him, but he seems to have done that pretty regularly. The 'Scouts' prizes' entry is straightforward enough: there was some kind of fête run by the Boy Scouts and he was to be at the prize-giving. Mrs. Acres says that he went and that nothing out of the ordinary happened. The last entry is perhaps the most interesting: 'N.B. Tell Mrs. Acres about Sarah White.' What about it, Jack?"

"Well, sir, Sarah White says that she wanted to borrow some collection of pressed flowers that Mrs. Acres has, because she wanted to use them to show her class in a nature lesson. Mrs. Acres agrees that she has the things, but can't remember being asked about them."

"Not necessarily significant, from what we've heard of the old man's memory. Still, he did write it down."

"It's a funny way to put it, though," Springer said. "If he meant to ask about flowers, why didn't he say so?"

"Yes, it is unusual. But as Mrs. Acres claims not to remember being told anything about Miss White, we're not much farther forward. Yet he did scrawl that phrase for a purpose. Confound this case! There's no lack of clues, but they lead nowhere."

"We'll puzzle it out in time, sir," Springer said cheerfully. "At least it looks as if Farrow, Malving and Sarah White are worth watching, but my money's still on Farrow. All we want now is a nice, juicy motive."

"I wish I knew what had happened to those books," Montero said, following his own line of thought. "From what Ludlow says, one of them might be coveted by the gang which has been playing its dirty tricks in the church, and another is rare enough for anyone's attention. Now it's clear that the Vicar meant to hide them somewhere and left a note to remind himself where. But what did he mean?"

"I don't reckon to be an expert on codes and things," Springer said, "and any bloke who can make something out of IK69 is smarter than what I am. Do you think the murderer was after the rare one, got hold of it before the old Vicar could hide it, and killed him to get away with it?"

"It's possible, and it might supply a better motive than any we have so far, except for the mysterious nephew who had a good enough reason for speeding up his legacy. I wish we could get hold of him. Now he stands to gain by the book being found and sold. Admittedly he only gets a half, but the proceeds of an open sale would probably be more than twice what could be got illegally. You can't just turn up with a book of that rarity without someone asking questions. Yet anyone who gained nothing from the will might think it worth taking a risk. Well, let's keep searching."

CHAPTER EIGHT

There are waiting-rooms which menace the occupant with the threat of an ordeal to come, rooms that seem to smell of accumulated misery at the hands of the dentist or the employment officer. There are others, cold preludes to a long journey, which seem to have no identity of their own but to be made up of countless fragments from passing lives. In general they are poorly adapted for their purpose of making unfamiliar surroundings bearable at a time when there is nothing to do but wait. The room in which Ludlow was sitting did not encourage his volatile spirit to reach one of its peaks. For one thing, it was very small and there was no way of disposing himself on the hard wooden chair in a manner that gave adequate room for his long legs. The tiny floor was largely claimed by a desk at which a pink young man with pimples and a piously cold expression was chewing his nails and looking covertly at Ludlow while appearing to read some letters. The Guild of Saints Cyprian and Severus occupied two rooms as its headquarters, one for the Secretary and one which doubled for his assistant and for waiting.

What the furniture lacked in originality was made up

by the walls, which sprouted lithographs and statuettes in Anglo-Catholic profusion. Ludlow gazed at a pamphlet entitled *How an Englishman may loyally use his Rosary at Mattins and Evensong*, while a portrait of Pusey looked down on him with disapproval from behind. A bell rang penetratingly, startling both Ludlow and the pimply youth, who ought to have been used to it. The latter scuttled into the inner office and returned in a moment.

"Mr. Pike-Lacey will see you now," he announced, giving Ludlow something between a nod and a genuflection.

Aloysius Pike-Lacey was even taller and thinner than Ludlow, and wore a dark suit which accentuated his appearance. His face was pale and not without nobility, though his deep eyes looked wild and haunted. The problems of ecclesiastical nicety seemed to exude like an exhalation from his perfectly shaven cheeks and jaws. He extended a lean hand to Ludlow, drawing him with unexpected force towards the only vacant chair. The desk was covered with what appeared to be small saucers full of black crystals and powder. Ludlow, always wary of things scientific, looked anxious.

"Try this one," said Pike-Lacey, thrusting a saucer towards him.

Unsure whether to taste it or use it as snuff, Ludlow took a cautious smell and said that it seemed very satisfactory.

"One of the religious communities makes it up,"

Pike-Lacey explained. "I think it will do very well for the purpose which we have in mind. Ah, my friend, when will the sweet savour of incense again be sent up in every parish church throughout our land?"

Ludlow was not sure of the answer to that one, but at least he knew now what the stuff was and he has never been slow at making use of an opening to suit his purpose.

"I'm sure that your influence towards that happy day has been greatly strengthened by your new bequest. A time for rejoicing, my friend, were it not won in such unhappy circumstances."

His assumed manner made him laugh and in trying to turn it into a cough he blew a good deal of incense in all directions. The effect seemed to stimulate Pike-Lacey, who gave a panegyric on the late Vicar and an outline of what the Guild intended to do with the money.

"Were you surprised at what you got from his will?" Ludlow asked when he had got his breath back and found a lull.

"One knew of his interest, of course, and also that he was well blessed with this world's goods. One had not expected such generosity, nor, alas, that it should come thus."

"Whoever killed him was your benefactor," Ludlow said bluntly.

"I suppose so, but what a dreadful way of putting it." Pike-Lacey crossed himself fervently.

"Have you any idea who it might have been?"

"How could I know? The dear man had no enemy in the world. There were of course those who calumniated and persecuted him, but murder! May I ask, what is your interest in this, Mr. Ludlow?"

"I should like to know who killed the Vicar and why. Call it a love of truth, if you like. I thought I might learn something here, in a place which seems to have been close to his work and affection."

"So it was, so it was indeed. Are you, too, interested in our task?"

"I'm sure it performs a useful function," Ludlow said cautiously.

"You can have no idea of the need. Liberalism, Mr. Ludlow, Modernism, Reasonableness – those are the names by which they now walk. Ancient usages, traditional practices are the butt even of those who continue to hold office within the church. What do you think of the book of the Bishop of Sydenham? Heresy, my friend, rank heresy. Let us thank the saints for the few parishes where true light still burns."

"Not everybody seems to have approved of the late Vicar's practices so far as I can tell," Ludlow broke in, unaccustomed and unwilling to be talked at so long. "I understand that a Miss Mason is making objections to the will."

"That woman? I could tell you such stories of her, did not charity forbid. If I tell you that she is a close associate of Angus Sprott, you will know what conclusions to draw."

Ludlow did not know, but he mentally filed the name away for future reference.

"So you don't think that the Vicar was killed because of his ecclesiastical views?" he asked.

"Gracious me, no. Why, not even Sprott would descend to murder. Of course, if he *was* killed by a zealous heretic, it might make him a martyr. When, oh when, will our church claim the power to canonise?"

This was becoming too deep for Ludlow, who started to squeeze his way out of the office. Pike-Lacey pursued him with a handshake.

Having got little profit from one interview, Ludlow was inclined to put the case out of his mind and concentrate on the several professional duties that were clamouring for attention. Whether it was his boasted love of truth or simply the curiosity which Montero accused him of, the various problems refused to go away and the extracts from the Vicar's diary came out of his pocket several times while he was trying to concentrate on other things. That same evening, telling himself that it was time for some exercise and also for one of his explorations of the London which never ceased to amaze and delight him, he set out in the early dusk.

It needs neither magic nor psychology to explain the fact that he eventually found himself drifting into the church on which the whole story centred. A few subdued lights gleamed out through the coloured windows and made them lovely. The sound of Elizabethan madrigals at the open door made Ludlow enter briskly and with enthusiasm. A bespectacled young man with an old face was facing a semicircle of assorted singers, vigorously conducting with both his arms. Ludlow slipped into a back pew and closed his eyes. As the melodies flowed over him, he slipped out of time and lost the ugly, sentimental pictures around the place, forgot the straining mouths above buttoned raincoats.

He dreamed of that past age which he loved best, of the time when this Church of England was sorting out her allegiances, debating continually the seat of true authority. When those madrigals were composed a surplice was the occasion of controversy and a theological interpretation might be the cause of violence. How tame and respectable it had become – or had it? Did the outward serenity mask murder as well as sanctity? The singing stopped and he was recalled sharply to his purpose.

"May I congratulate you?" he murmured to the conductor, who was collecting the parts of music and giving final exhortations to his departing choir.

"Very kind of you – a bit unusual for us, but we're preparing for a special recital. I'm the organist of this church, by the way. Are you new to the parish?"

"I've been to this church once or twice before," Ludlow said vaguely.

"I hope you'll come to our little recital. The collection will be in aid of the roof. We need all the support we can get."

"Support for the recital or for the roof?"

"Well, they go together really. There are some terrible weaknesses in the plaster up there – it was shaken in the war and we've never really got it put right. The whole thing will be down on our heads one day."

Both men looked anxiously upwards for a few seconds.

"The church has suffered a lot recently," Ludlow said, probing. "This bad news about the roof comes on top of the various sacrileges that have taken place. I hope the police will get to the root of them soon."

"I don't believe they're trying," the organist said with an indignant flash of his glasses. "If they knew their business, the poor Vicar would never have been killed. I could tell them where to look, but nobody takes any notice of what I say."

"Where?" Ludlow asked, almost pushing the pathetic organist over in his excitement.

"There are some very queer things happening in that old, empty house in the street behind the church. The one next to the open space. I've seen some very odd-looking people going in there when I've passed it after choir-practice. It's my belief that all the trouble comes from there."

"Do you mean that there's some kind of Satanism being practised in that house?"

"It feels evil, that's all I know. Good night."

The organist broke away abruptly, looking pale and frightened. Dropping a perfunctory knee to the altar, he disappeared out of the door and into the night which was now quite dark. Ludlow walked thoughtfully after him, with the vague feeling that things were beginning to show the outlines of a pattern. Shapes out of the confusion formed and disappeared without trace, but perhaps the day's work had not been in vain.

He realised that once again he was not alone in the church. A woman was standing by one of the pillars, gazing at him but seeming to see something far beyond him. She was not in her first youth, but there was a prettiness approaching beauty in the small face under auburn hair and in her slim figure. Seen motionless in that setting, she might herself have been a statue or a figure from a picture: perhaps a woman facing martyrdom, for there was deep fear in her eyes.

Although a firm and well-tried bachelor, Ludlow is much more susceptible to women than he would admit even to himself. In fact, he has been sadly taken in more than once by an appearance of helplessness. He was struggling between his compassion for the woman's obvious distress and his own reticence about intruding, when the question was resolved by a deep sob. Her eyes were wet when he tentatively moved towards her; she was no longer a pictured martyr, but a living and very human being.

"Is there anything I can do?" Ludlow asked gently.

The woman looked at him, first with a vague surprise that there should be anyone there at all, and then with something close to repulsion. She put out her arm as if to ward him off, shook her head and stumbled blindly towards the door. While Ludlow stood wondering whether to follow, he heard voices in the porch outside and a moment later Malving came in and strode up the aisle towards him.

"Ah, Mr. Malving," Ludlow said. "I've just been listening to your excellent choir rehearsing."

"Yes – yes, they're very good."

The Curate looked worried and unwilling to stop, but Ludlow went on with the confidence of those who have enjoyed for too long the lecturer's privilege of uninterrupted discourse.

"That woman who just went out – you must have seen her – she seemed very distressed about something. Do you think we ought to go after her and see if we can help?"

"Oh, I know her. It was Sarah White, the secretary of our P.C.C. I'm sure there's nothing wrong with her at all. Excuse me, please."

Malving went off abruptly in the direction of the vestry. There was no sign of the woman in the dark street when Ludlow got outside, and he walked away wondering what that brief encounter had meant. Was Malving really so heartless, or so lacking in perception? The opinions of all those who knew his pastoral work seemed to deny it, but what other explanation could there be? Even when Ludlow was back in the glorious untidiness of his own flat and had poured himself a drink, he was still troubled by a vision of auburn hair and of a face that seemed to carry more sorrow than any woman should have to endure.

"That seems to put paid to Farrow," Montero said. His expression did not show the satisfaction which the words suggested, and Springer too was frowning and pulling at his lower lip. On the desk in front of them were spread out several account-books, bank-records, and a few neatly typed sheets of official paper.

"I don't reckon to understand all the figures, sir," Springer said. "I've got a feeling those ruddy accountants of ours are doing me every time I get my pay – bits off for this and bits off for that all the time. But this lot makes sense right enough. Farrow's been larking with the books and putting the collections into his own little pocket."

"That's about it, Jack, though it's more serious than collections – there are a few trust funds attached to the parish that aren't straight either. Farrow's own finances are in a pretty mess after he lost heavily on some stupid investments, and he was trying to put them right before the audit. It's the old story, of course. The gambler never believes he can lose, any more than the crook ever believes that he can get caught. It doesn't matter whether it's a shilling on the pools or a couple of thousand on the Stock Exchange – it's always going to be all right next time."

"But the Vicar got wise to it, and had to be bumped off."

"And that ought to be the end of this case. But we may have a job proving that the Vicar did know, because the old man seems to have been like a child about money. Still, he had the sense to make a will, so perhaps he wasn't so dim after all. He scrawled a few words on his diary that pointed to a date when Farrow had called to see him. So now we pull in Farrow, he's sent for trial and the case is closed. Any comments?"

Springer made a face and tapped one of the books on the desk as if he would make it give up its secret like an oracle.

"It don't sound so good as it ought to, sir," he confessed. "If the old man had the strength to write at all after he was shot, why didn't he just write Farrow's name? And the twenty-third of July wasn't the only date that Farrow was down in the diary. What made him think of it just at that time when he was going off?"

"That entry won't stand up for a moment in court, and we both know it. There's as much evidence in it against Malving, or Sarah White, or Mrs. Acres."

"Or the blooming Boy Scouts," Springer said gloomily.

"Yet something must have fixed that date in his mind. It may be something not connected with the diary itself at all. So we're back at square one."

"Not quite, sir. I mean, Farrow had a fair old motive."

"Yes, and in desperation he may have killed the Vicar to stave off the time when the audit would show up everything. But there are so many things that don't seem to fit. Why didn't Farrow clear off as soon as he'd done it instead of hanging about for an hour? The quacks are certain that the Vicar was killed no later than seven-thirty. And why did he take the enormous risk of putting his gun back in the vestry instead of throwing it away, which would have made it look much more as though someone had stolen it? He must have done it early the next morning, because we kept him until late, and Blanch was on watch in the church after that."

"Maybe Blanch is in it too. I mean, he's a friend of our Mr. Ludlow, and you know what them professors can get up to. Then Malving took the early service, and he might have helped him to smuggle it in. Remember, the old Vicar had been made to climb down about getting him a house."

Montero banged on the desk with a vigour that would have alarmed anyone except the sergeant who knew him so well, and swore with a fluency ripened by being seldom practised. He wrote the name "Farrow" in capital letters on a piece of paper, drew a circle around it and then crossed it out.

"We shan't be able to make it stick," he said. "The very fact that Farrow made no secret of having the gun is the first thing that a sharp Counsel will pounce on. We may see it as double bluff, but will a jury? Let's start from there. Farrow brought out the gun and put it in the church because of breaking-in by some kind of Satanists. And that was the case we were originally called in to deal with. Perhaps we'd better get back to it, because there's more than likely to be a connection. One at least of the Vicar's books would mean a lot to people of that sort."

"We're no wiser to solving the crossword puzzle about where the Vicar put them," Springer said.

"Not an inch. I was hoping that Ludlow might come up with something. He's good at that kind of game. I hope he's not trying to solve this thing on his own, or he may walk into more than he bargained for."

"There's not a trace of that Tom Finchley, either."

"Nor there is. We'll have to step up the pressure on that, because he's got the best motive of all so far — quick money. That makes two missing men in this blasted case — unless they turn out to be only one."

"Who's the other, sir?"

"The Unknown Penitent. Who was the Vicar waiting for, to hear a special confession? That person might be able to tell us a lot."

The two detectives looked again at the mess of papers. This time it was Springer who did the swearing; he did it lengthily and without repeating himself.

CHAPTER NINE

The Reverend Alexander Twotten blew out his cheeks in a manner which had often been gleefully imitated by the small boys at a certain mission school in East Africa. At the present moment he felt deeply nostalgic for the field of service overseas which he had only recently left for the sake of his health. To fill in as the temporary vicar of a parish before the new appointment was made could never be regarded as the ideal occupation, though it was a reasonable and indeed welcome way of looking around for employment somewhere in the church at home. But when the vacancy had been caused by the sudden and violent death of the previous incumbent, when the parish church had been defiled by some kind of Satanic practice and when the parish affairs had been dragged into newspaper publicity, he felt justified in regarding himself as less than the most fortunate of men.

The morning had started with a visit from Miss Mason, bearing with her a long list of grievances and illegal practices which he was supposed to stop without delay. Alexander Twotten himself was of the moderately high persuasion, and although he had shaken his head over a few of the things which he had discovered on first coming into the parish church, he was not disposed to make any great changes during his short tenancy. But there was Miss Mason, holding forth about archdeacons, and faculties, and ecclesiastical law and such other matters as it was scarcely proper for a layman – and still for a laywoman – to meddle with. Twotten sat and groaned within himself until she took her leave, abandoning him to feeling that he must be something like one of the wicked priests in Foxe's *Book of Martyrs*.

Now there was this business with Malving. The young curate sat opposite him, looking apologetic but also a little defiant. A very good fellow, Twotten thought, much better than they tended to send from the theological colleges nowadays. Yet there was no escaping the horror that lay displayed on the table between the two clergymen. For the tenth time that morning, Twotten read a passage in the same paper which had caused such a stir at the P.C.C. meeting only a little time ago:

"There's a young curate who's hoping to get married quite soon. Lucky fellow, you say? Not so lucky after all. He's feeling worried because he's got nowhere to bring his bride for their first home together.

But doesn't the Church of England provide homes for its parsons? Oh yes, there's a house all right – just the sort of place for a young couple. But he can't have it! Why? Because it's already occupied and nobody seems to be willing to do anything about it.

Of course, it may just be one of those funny coincidences

that the present occupant is the niece of the Archdeacon of Wapping. But somehow we find that pretty hard to believe.

The Church of England seems to care more for its rich leaders than for the poor chaps who do the real work. The ordinary man who believes in English Fair Play will be wondering whether this is the Church for him."

"I'm terribly sorry," Malving said. "I'd no idea the chap was going to make a story out of it – he seemed really interested in the church and all that was going on, and anyway I didn't say anything about being dissatisfied with the decision. And it's not long since they were blaming me for wanting the house, so they can't have it both ways."

"Unfortunately they can." Twotten blew out his cheeks again and sadly scratched his chin while Malving sat with his hands in his lap and tried to look attentive.

"The world at large," he went on, "never finds any difficulty in attacking the Church. Whatever decisions are made in her name will be given a bad interpretation by those whose minds are already made up. There is no other institution that is simultaneously accused of going to so many contrary extremes, and all of them wrong. While that goes on, she at least proves that she's alive, so we won't worry too much."

Anyone who stands outside a university college about the time when lectures are ending for the day might form a curious impression of the men and women who attempt to instruct the young. Bulging under shabby raincoats and hats, or shapeless beneath overcoats that hang too loosely, the staff tend to look as if they were coming away from an issue of old clothes by a benevolent but not very well-endowed mission. Ludlow is not one of those who raise the general standard, and he increases the basic effect of being unemployable by his habit of walking with his eyes fixed on the ground while he is thinking.

On this evening he was thinking hard as he came out of his college, damply plunging into the gathering mist and squelching along the pavement which seemed to have accumulated the dirt of several generations in one day. His battered briefcase contained sandwiches, an unusual thing for one who likes his food and can seldom be diverted from a full and prolonged meal. Now, however, he had different plans, which were likely to take up a good deal of time.

Ludlow was only a few yards away from his underground station when he became aware of someone walking in step with him about two feet behind his right shoulder. This presence had been vaguely troubling him ever since he left the college, but had not fully broken into his thoughts. Now, however, it quickened its pace, drew round him and blocked his way. Ludlow came to a jerky stop and glared at the impediment. It was the man who had come to see him with cryptic questions about old books, the man whom Montero's detective had shadowed and lost.

"Fancy running into you again." The man grinned cheekily and looked at Ludlow as if he were an old friend.

The tide of homegoing humanity surged and battled around them, grabbing newspapers before the descent into the earth. Ludlow gripped his briefcase and tried to think out a plan of action.

"I think we've met before," he said.

"You bet we have. Any luck with old books lately?"

"I'm afraid I don't know what you mean."

"Oh, we all know that you're interested in old books. Some of them turn out to be quite valuable. You don't waste your time with cheap stuff. I admire you for that, Mr. Ludlow. I like a man who can tell me whether the things I've got are worth anything or not. I'm in the selling business myself and I appreciate a man who knows a good bargain. Yes, I really do appreciate a man like that."

"I'm afraid you didn't have anything of value," Ludlow said, looking round for a policeman and not finding one.

"I know, I know. I just don't have any luck with things like that. Not like some people. Now I had a relation who died recently, and he seemed to have a real gift for getting value in old books. Some said it was luck and some said that the old man was craftier than he gave out, but anyway he got himself some very nice stuff indeed. Worth a lot of money, they say."

"What happened to his library after he died?"

Ludlow asked, feeling that the whole thing was unreal yet somehow important.

"Now that's a very good question. What did happen to it? There's someone who knows the answer, but it isn't me. It might be Overley, mightn't it, because he's in the business? It might be your colleague Cyril Blanch, who started taking an interest in old books all of a sudden. Or it might very well be you, Mr. Ludlow."

"Or it might be Tom Finchley," Ludlow said with reckless inspiration. The other man shook his head.

"Not me," he said. "If I knew, I wouldn't be asking you."

"You are Tom Finchley, then?"

"Sure I am. Didn't I ever introduce myself – I'm so sorry, how frightfully remiss of me."

He looked unabashed, seeming to mock Ludlow's speech and accent. Ludlow made a vague movement towards him then reflected that it was foolish and probably illegal to seize a man who showed no sign of running away. They stood facing each other while the rush-hour crowd thickened around them.

"If your uncle had any books of great value, it will mean a lot of money for you," Ludlow said.

"And I need that money. Ludlow, you don't know how much I need every bit of it."

"Your uncle's death must have been a shock to you, Finchley," said Ludlow, who hates the use of his untitled surname by strangers.

"It was too bad about the old boy. He never had much

time for me, you know, but he said he'd see me all right when he died. It's going to be just too bad if anyone's pinched some of his most valuable books."

"I doubt whether anything has been purloined. Your uncle seems to have put his latest purchase of books in a safe place, and no doubt it will be found." Ludlow was thinking hard and suddenly decided what to do. "Look here, why not come back to my flat? We can have a drink and talk over the situation, and I'll get in touch with someone who may be able to help you."

Finchley seemed pleased to come, and eventually they emerged from the ordeal of public transport and settled down in Ludlow's untidy but comfortable flat. Ludlow felt a little anxious about his own boldness, but Finchley was apparently relaxed and willing to stay indefinitely. Fortunately, the telephone was not in the main room. Trying to lower his normally penetrating voice, Ludlow dialled to Scotland Yard and asked for Montero. The inspector had gone home, but fortunately Ludlow had his number and was able to reach him. The conversation that followed would have taxed the patience of anyone less quick-witted than Montero, or of anyone less accustomed to Ludlow.

When Ludlow returned to his guest, Finchley had made himself comfortable by putting his feet up among some of the papers which were in a system clear and precious to Ludlow but to nobody else. He was smoking and dropping the ash on the floor, so that it was only with a stern remembrance of the duty to further the ends of justice that Ludlow was able civilly to offer him a drink.

"Scotch will do me, old man," Finchley said cheerfully, "and you needn't drown it."

Ludlow grudgingly poured out a large measure of whisky and took one for himself. Since Finchley was in the best chair, he lowered his long body cautiously on to a stool and tried to look genial. The effect was that of a crocodile on holiday, but Finchley seemed happy with it. Their wristwatches ticked loudly in the silence, and Ludlow wondered how to keep his unwelcome visitor until Montero came.

"You've got a nice lot of books here," Finchley said. "Any of them worth much?"

Ludlow never needs any encouragement to talk about his books and he started producing some of his treasures. Finchley waved them aside and flicked his ash over a fine leather binding.

"It's the sixteenth-century stuff that really makes money, isn't it?" he said with a leer.

"That largely depends on its rarity." Ludlow had his back to Finchley and was making hideous faces at the opposite wall.

"So they tell me. I mean, if there were only one copy of something and then another one turned up, it would be worth quite a bit. Tell me, Ludlow, what would you do if you found a book like that?"

"I should see that it went to its rightful owner," Ludlow said.

"Still, it might be a temptation, mightn't it? If nobody knew where the book was, and if the bloke who'd bought it had popped off and couldn't say – well, who's to know if it's just written off as lost? But if someone who knows about books – someone like yourself for instance – happens to come upon it, what's to stop him from keeping it or selling it?"

"Some people are not motivated by dishonest greed, though that is something which you may find it difficult to grasp."

Ludlow sounded more priggish than righteous and his face was pale with anger. Finchley grinned as if a good joke had been made, then stretched himself and dropped his cigarette into the hearth.

"Well, I must shove off," he said. "Duty calls, and all that. It's been nice talking to you. We must get together again some time."

"No, don't go," Ludlow said desperately. "Have some more whisky. I particularly want you to meet my friend who's coming soon."

Finchley shrugged and held out his glass. The two men sank back into a hostile silence, though Finchley continued to look amused.

"It was very sad about your uncle," Ludlow said after a time. "His sudden death came when he was worried about the outbreaks of Satanism that had desecrated the church."

"Oh yes, I heard something about it. What exactly do those characters reckon they're doing?"

As comfortably as the low stool would permit, Ludlow settled himself to give a lecture.

"The kind of Satanism that sometimes appears in western countries today probably springs from the activities of sensation-seeking decadents in France and elsewhere during the last century, but its true origins are much older. Call it Satanism, Black Magic, or Witchcraft – I don't claim to be an anthropologist and no doubt some of my colleagues would rebuke my careless terminology – but in any case it goes back to the Middle Ages and probably before. Some authorities see it as an anti-Christian movement connected with certain heresies, while others believe it to be a survival of the pre-Christian pagan religions that were concerned with fertility and sympathetic magic. In the shadows of history it is difficult to discover the truth, but two facts seem indisputable. One is that a lot of innocent people suffered because the power of the witch was so much feared. The other is that modern outbreaks are nearly always an excuse for orgies."

"What like?" asked Finchley, showing interest for the first time.

"Ranging from sexual promiscuity to murder. The choice of a church shows the quasi-religious cover that is adopted. At one time, a renegade priest would invert his sacred power and lead the blasphemous ceremonies —"

Ludlow stopped and looked excited as if a new thought had come to him. Then he shook his head and went on with his explanation. He had digressed into ghosts, by way of poltergeists and familiar spirits, when there was an imperious ring at the doorbell. Leaving his discourse unfinished, an unusual concession for him, he leapt up and went to admit Montero. The inspector walked straight in without greeting him and stood in the doorway of the living-room.

"Are you Thomas Finchley?" he asked

"That's right, old man," Finchley said, not getting out of his chair. "My pals call me Tom. Come along and have a noggin – old Ludlow keeps quite a decent Scotch."

"I am Inspector Montero of the C.I.D. and I should like to ask you a few questions. We've been looking for you for some time."

"Have you really? It's rather nice to find that someone's interested in me at last. The world in general seems to be quite lacking in interest."

"Why haven't you come forward?" Montero said sternly.

"I don't follow you, old man."

"All the newspapers have carried appeals for you to get in touch with us to help with our inquiries into the murder of your uncle."

"I never have time to read the papers. Still, here I am, but it won't do you any good."

"What do you mean by that?" asked Montero.

"I know what you mean by helping with your inquiries. You want to make out that it was I who did for the old chap. Well, it wasn't and I've got an alibi, so put that in your pipe and smoke it, copper."

"Do you feel like telling me where you were on the evening when your uncle was killed?" Montero asked without a flicker of annoyance.

"Sure. I was at a conference with all the lads who work the same area as me – selling round the houses, you know. All the things the housewife dreams of – why should the neighbours have what you haven't got? Easy terms after three days' free trial —"

"All right, Finchley, you're not going to sell me anything. What was this conference?"

"Every month the Area Supervisor gets us together – no overtime for the evening of course, but you've got to be there, or else. You ought to see one of them. God, it's a right laugh with their pep-talks and new sales gimmicks, and the knife in your guts if you've dropped below your quota."

"I shall check on your story. Now, have you any objection to accompanying me for further inquiries?"

"Anything to oblige a copper. But I've got a fair way to go and work tomorrow. What about laying on some transport home?"

"We'll get you home, if we're satisfied."

Finchley smiled sleepily and heaved himself out of his chair. He handed Ludlow his empty glass and looked at him with something like affection.

"That wasn't a very nice trick, Ludlow," he said. "Fancy asking a chap in for a drink and then putting the coppers on to him. No, that wasn't a very nice trick at all. It's a good job I've got nothing to hide, isn't it?"

"Come on," Montero said sharply. "Thanks. I'll get in touch," he added to Ludlow.

When they had gone, Ludlow took the sandwiches out of his briefcase and started chewing them. He looked even more abstracted than usual as he wandered about the flat, with a drink in one hand, and muttered to himself through the breadcrumbs. Had one the right to play the part of justice, to trap a fellow human being just because his manner was offensive and one leapt to the suspicion of guilt? If Finchley had been more agreeable, would he have been so anxious to do Montero's work for him? But there was another job to be undertaken now, alone; and meanwhile the doubts must be left to those whose profession was to deal with them. Ludlow had one more drink, put on his outdoor clothes again, cast a regretful look around the comfortable room and went out.

The night had got much colder and he shivered in spite of the whisky as he made his way along the street outside. There were few people about in this dead time when the homegoing workers had gone and the pleasure-seekers had not yet emerged from pubs and cinemas. When at last he reached the district that had occupied so much of his time in the past few days, the gritty dampness seemed to eat into him and warn him that he was walking to destruction. He impatiently shrugged the idea away, but his spirits drooped and only a mixture of pride and curiosity kept him from turning back.

Darkness was kind to the church, which lost its fussiness in silhouette and presented lines that were not unpleasing against the night sky. From there he had no difficulty in following what the organist had told him and finding the deserted house. It was in a street of houses whose florid but shabby red-brick fronts barely held up the stretches of shoddy Victorian building behind. It was difficult to tell which were empty and which merely neglected and uncurtained, but the one which he sought proclaimed its dereliction like a beggar. The railings had long since gone and the low stone coping was cracked in several places. There were more gaps than tiles in the horrid mosaic path that led to the hole which had once held a front door.

Ludlow stood in the hall, suffering one of the periods of fierce self-deprecation which alternate with his normally good opinion of himself. He was really the most foolish of men, a disgrace to his profession, one who should never for a moment fancy himself as a detective. He might as well go back and hide his shame. In the excitement, he had forgotten to bring an electric torch.

Yet even as he stood in the darkness and cursed himself, there came a feeling of not being entirely alone. The house which had seemed deserted began to smell and feel strangely inhabited. He edged his way along the slimy wall until his hand reached vacancy. Very cautiously striking a match, he found himself to be at the top of a narrow flight of stairs into the basement regions, from which there came a low murmur of voices. It did not sound like connected conversations, but rather as if several people were talking independently, starting and breaking off without regard for the others. Occasionally there was an unpleasant kind of laugh.

Ludlow started down the stairs, reflecting that he was in a well-policed city. Even so, there was something uncanny about the bursts of noise that punctuated the dark silence. Was it not this very lack of order, this breaking of normal patterns, which was supposed to be a characteristic of Black Magic? He wondered whether there was more than human evil to meet, whether some monstrous power was raised and gathered here. A thin line of light came under a closed door not far from the bottom of the stairs. Chiding himself for superstition, Ludlow forced his feet to go on. The strange noises grew louder. He was just going to strike another match when something cold closed tightly around his neck.

CHAPTER TEN

Ludlow stood in the darkness, gulping as hard as the pressure on his neck allowed. Behind the closed door, the noise continued to rise and fall as before. The sense of evil weighed down the air all round him and seemed to add its own smell to the unmistakeable dampness of decaying woodwork. A voice that seemed human told him not to move, but at the same time the coldness at the back of his neck increased and propelled him forwards. Between these contrary indications, he soon found himself with his nose against the door and unable to make any further progress. The pressure relaxed a little and the door was suddenly pushed open.

The light in the basement room came only from candles and one smoky oil-lamp, but after the few minutes of absolute darkness it was enough to make Ludlow blink and fail to distinguish things clearly. Gradually he realised with some relief that the occupants, though far from prepossessing, were apparently not supernatural. They were sitting all around the walls on upturned boxes, or sprawled on piles of sacking. There were in fact only a few of them, mostly young and all dirty, but they looked like a multitude in the flickering light. The illusion was increased by the fact that they seemed to be holding desultory conversations and private monologues without taking much notice of each other.

The force which had propelled him along the passage was now revealed to be a large young man, probably no older than many of the students he was accustomed to teach, but more uncouth than even the worst of them. The hand which still kept a clammy grip on his neck was strong and dirty; the bare forearm which led from it to a blue woollen jersey was dotted with little red marks like insect bites. A tall girl, so thin and pale that she might have been one of the spirits of Ludlow's earlier imaginings, with long greasy hair falling across her face, swayed towards him and looked pleadingly into his eyes.

"Have you got it?" she asked.

Ludlow shook his head so vigorously that he got his neck free and was able to turn and look at the man behind him. The face that he saw was heavily bearded, the lips full and sensual, the eyes those of a madman or a saint. Relieved to find no more unusual opponents, Ludlow was about to demand some explanations when the thin girl began to moan and sob, pleading with him for something that he could not understand. Sweat broke out on her face, while her teeth began to chatter as if she were having a fit. With a horror that swamped all his notions of witchcraft, Ludlow suddenly understood her anguish and also the red marks on the young man's arm. No magic rituals offered them escape from reality:

if they worshipped the devil, they did it in the form of drugs.

The young man took the girl savagely by the shoulder and pushed her away. She crawled like an animal to the far end of the wall and crouched there sobbing. Nobody took any notice of her, but a very small man with a broad face that twitched from a grin to a scowl and back all the time, came and stood in front of Ludlow.

"Now talk," said the bearded man.

"I shan't talk if I don't want to," Ludlow said petulantly. "What do you mean by this outrageous behaviour?" He glared as if at a delinquent student.

"What do *you* mean by shoving in here?"

"I lost my way. I appear to be in the wrong house. I was on my way to dine with friends and I must have gone in by the wrong gate."

It sounded unconvincing even to him. The small man poked him in the stomach and made him bend forward involuntarily. The bearded man seized him by the neck again and hauled him upright.

"This really won't do," Ludlow said. "And if you think I'm going to let you manhandle me like this you're greatly mistaken. If it's money you want, let me tell you —"

"We don't want money – not from your sort." The small man spoke savagely and poked again but Ludlow evaded him.

"What do you want then?"

"Tell him, Rodney."

The small man looked almost with reverence at his bearded companion, who smiled and suddenly looked gentle.

"We want to be left alone," he said. "We want to do things our own way, not because the rest of society does them. We don't like society and we claim the right to contract out of the rat-race and the bombs and the bloody politicians who'd rather die than live. And if we contract out of the things you reckon to be good, we may lose some of the things we like as well, but that's part of the bargain and we stick to it. Now go back to your little semi-detached villa, and draw your cretonne curtains and tell the others about what you've seen and can't understand. Get out, and leave us in peace."

His voice was pleasant and educated; he spoke like a man uttering a creed of which he was proud. Ludlow lost his anger and a good deal of his confidence. There was pity certainly, but the rejection of pity by its objects left him for once with nothing to say. He turned and walked back into the darkness of the passage, his eyes searching for the grey patch that led to the easier darkness of the night outside. The man called Rodney followed him in silence, not touching him. At the broken doorstep Ludlow tried to do something about the first purpose of his visit.

"I'm rather interested in the church in the next road," he said. "I wonder whether you could tell me —"

"We can't tell you anything about churches. They

may have a language, but it isn't ours. The clergy preach against us, and we can only spit. They're fools or crooks, perhaps both."

"The clergy around here do more work in a week than you've done in your whole life. By what right do you stand there and malign a dedicated and underpaid body of men, who know the meaning of unselfishness and service? If you don't speak their language as you put it, so much the worse for you."

Ludlow was surprised by his own vehemence. The moment of pity for that inverted creed was over. Perhaps there was boredom and insecurity in the ages of witchcraft too, driving men and women to the same attempts to escape as lead them now to drugs. Rodney looked hard at him, and looked with eyes that made Ludlow seem by far the younger of the two.

"Live with your dreams, little man," Rodney said. "You ask about the church. If you saw the clergy here as we do, peering out of the darkness at them when they don't know, you'd have a different idea. The young one, the curate or whatever he is, down in the shadows by the churchyard with a woman. And the same night, the old man's shot down like a gangster. Go to Heaven with that mob if you like, but I'll go to Hell with my own."

"Just a minute," Ludlow said, forgetting both his fear and his anger. "What time in the evening was this?"

"There's no time here, dad. It was dark, like it always is when the sun goes down."

Rodney's eyes looked wilder and sweat broke out on

his face. Ludlow stepped out and went quickly to the street, torn between pity and revulsion. The Satanists had not revealed themselves, but the equally upleasant encounter had not been entirely wasted.

"Have a fag, mate," said Detective Sergeant Springer.

The darkness outside the small window was giving way to a grey hint of autumnal dawn. Tom Finchley rubbed his hand over his face and thankfully reached for a cigarette. He showed the effects of continuous questioning, but had not lost the cocksure jauntiness which had so annoyed Ludlow. Montero had slammed the door only a few minutes before and now Springer was looking benevolent and lounging back in his chair as if the whole thing were a bore. Not being one of the regular clients of the Metropolitan Police, Finchley seemed to be accepting the different attitudes at their surface value. Montero and Springer had their own agreed signals for passing on a tough or gentle attitude when one relieved the other at interrogation.

"Is he always such a bastard?" Finchley asked.

"He's a tough one, and specially when he's been up all night. If he comes back to you again, you'll wish you'd never been born," said Springer, cheerfully maligning his chief in a good cause.

"What's he want to know then? I've told him all there is to tell. Won't he leave me alone unless I give myself in for a murder I never did?"

"You're holding out on something, and he knows it. I don't know, because I don't reckon to be so clever as what the inspector is. But if you come clean with me, it'll do me a bit of good and I can make it easier for you."

Springer leaned forward eagerly, with a look of complete innocence on his well-trained face. Finchley ground out his unfinished cigarette and looked down at the bare table that separated them.

"I've nothing more to tell you," he said.

"Let's go over a few things again," Springer said as if Finchley had not spoken. "When you went to see Mr. Ludlow first of all, why didn't you tell him who you were?"

"Why should I?" The cheekiness was suddenly back in Finchley's face and voice; he seemed amused at something.

"It's the usual thing, isn't it, when you meet a bloke?"

"Maybe it is in your business, not in mine. You learn not to give everything away. I went to ask his advice about some old books. What do names matter?"

"You had his name all right, though. How did you find out about him?"

"I get around."

"If you get around so much, how come you never heard that we were wanting to interview you?"

"I don't mix with blokes who read the police news. I'm particular about the company I keep."

Springer breathed hard down his nose but did not change his expression or his tone.

"I believe you knew about it," he said, "and for some reason were afraid to come forward. What was it?"

"Prove it."

"We will, don't worry. But in any case, when you knew your uncle had been murdered, why didn't you come and talk to us of your own accord?"

"Why should I? Look, I was sorry about the old boy, but I couldn't care less what happens now. Neither does he, and we can't do anything for him. Let it go. Now you tell me something. Have I ever once denied being Tom Finchley? And have I ever tried to cut and run? I've gone on with my job like a good citizen, haven't I? That's not what a murderer does, you know."

"I don't need you to tell me nothing about murderers," said Springer, forgetting his friendly role for the moment. "You've got a lot of explaining to do, and you'd better get on with it before Inspector Montero comes back. We've got enough on you already —"

"It's a waste of time asking questions then, isn't it?" Finchley yawned and looked at the lightening greyness outside the window. "You coppers always pretend to know it all so that you can get a confession. It's one of the oldest tricks in the business, but it doesn't fool me. You don't even know what the message in the diary means."

"How do you know about that?" Springer looked like a lean gun-dog about to seize a fallen bird.

"I thought you had all the answers. You tell me, mate."

"How do you know?" Springer was on his feet and leaning across the table.

"I've stopped talking. Tell the inspector we might as well all go home. I'm just bored with the whole lot of you."

Finchley slumped forward on the table and started to snore with artificial loudness. Springer glared at him, clenched his fists but restrained himself and went to report to Montero.

"I haven't much opinion of the morals of travelling salesmen," Montero said thoughtfully, "but I doubt whether a couple of dozen of them could all be persuaded to cover up for a murderer. We know already from phoning the area manager that the conference was held on that evening, and that Finchley was there from seven till ten. We'll have to get hold of the other fellows for confirmation, but there doesn't seem to be any doubt of it. Finchley is nicely covered for the whole period."

"But he's as guilty as hell, sir," Springer protested. "He's been laughing up his sleeve at us all the time. He stands to gain by the will – and how does he know about what was written in the diary?"

"Yes, that slip would be good enough if he didn't have what seems to be a cast-iron alibi. We haven't let out that bit of news to anyone."

"Mr. Ludlow knows about it, sir."

"Yes, confound his interfering mind. He may have let it out to Finchley when they were together during the evening. I warned him not to get mixed up in things he couldn't stop. We'll have to ask him."

"If he didn't say anything, that's it, then."

"You think so, Jack, and I think so. But what's the good of charging Finchley? We'd never even get him committed for trial if he could produce an alibi with that number of witnesses. We've got to break his alibi before we can charge him, and we can't keep him here indefinitely without charging him."

"So we let him go, sir?"

"So we let him go, and keep him under observation. What else can we do?"

"What about Farrow, then? Is he in the clear?"

"Nobody's clear until the case is solved. No, we go on investigating. But we're not doing any more before breakfast."

From inside Montero's office, the sky did not look much brighter three hours later, though the night had given way to a depressing November day that almost concealed one side of the river from the other. Looking as fresh as if he had had a good night's sleep, but betrayed by the dark shadows around his eyes, Montero was poring over a document that Springer had just laid before him. The handwriting experts had been working on the Vicar's diary. His last message was in such a hopeless scrawl that it was impossible to relate it to any other specimens. There was a long straggling tail on the

'Re', a tail which the experts thought might represent a feeble attempt to make a 'g'.

"Reg July 23," Springer said. "Now who the heck is Reg? I don't believe that there's a single Reginald among them."

Montero was staring hard at the paper in front of him. Suddenly he got up, seized his coat and hat and rushed out of the office. Springer trotted loyally after him.

"What's up, then?" he asked plaintively as they went down the stairs. "Where are we going, sir?"

"We're going to the church, quickly. It's clear enough now. What the old man wrote was 'Reg July 23' – Reg was as far as he could get with Register. There's something for that date in the church register of marriages and baptisms, and the sooner we find it the better. Come on!"

They were at the church very soon, but were not the first visitors there that morning. The sound of a familiar voice, only slightly subdued in deference to the surroundings, greeted them as they came through the door. Ludlow was in earnest conversation with Twotten at the foot of the stairs leading up to the gallery. The conjunction of a lecturer and a clergyman is a formidable one, since both are generally accustomed to speaking for long periods without interruption. When Montero and Springer came into the church, Ludlow seemed to be winning.

"In considering any aspect of the various shades of opinion within the Church of England today," he was saying, "we see reflected some phase of her history. As a teacher of English literature, I continually need to remind my students of the part which the parish church has played in the lives of the people —"

"You're up early this morning," Montero said before Ludlow could give Twotten any more instruction about his own church.

"I don't know what gives you the idea that you get up before anyone else," Ludlow said. "I was actually here for the early service, and Mr. Twotten has kindly been telling me some things about the church. Anyway, you look as if you hadn't been to bed at all."

"We haven't." Montero turned to Twotten. "I'm glad to see you, sir, because we need your help. Can we have a look at the parish register?"

"You can safely show it to him," Ludlow said. "Inspector Montero is an old acquaintance of mine, and I'm sure that he would not do any damage to your property."

Montero glared at him, then ostentatiously turned his back and explained to Twotten what they wanted. Ludlow listened with interest and followed the party when they went into the vestry. Nobody actually told him to leave, so he sat on the desk where Farrow dealt with the accounts and tucked his long legs out of the way as much as possible. The register was produced and Montero eagerly turned back the pages, then started to swear but looked hastily at Twotten and turned it into a cough.

There was no entry of any kind for the twenty-third

of July. The two detectives looked blankly at each other.

"Try a different year," said Ludlow, apparently interested only in his fingernails.

"He wouldn't have put a date like that without the year," Springer said. "Though of course he mightn't have been able to finish it. Have we got to go through every ruddy book in the place – I beg pardon, your reverence."

"No of course, Ludlow's right. It didn't stand for the twenty-third of July at all, but for July 1923. Could you possibly find the register for that year, sir?"

Since Twotten was not familiar with the places where things were kept, it took a little time to unearth the old register. As he turned rapidly to July, Montero recognised the Vicar's writing, a little firmer but without doubt the same as appeared in the diary. He had served the parish from youth to old age, until he was shot down without a moment to prepare for death. Montero's knuckles were white as he gripped the book but his face showed no emotion of anger or excitement. But he could not restrain a cry of triumph after he had scanned a few entries.

Tom Finchley had been christened by his uncle in July 1923. The name that had been occupying so much of Montero's thoughts stood out like an accusation on the page.

"That fixes it," Springer said.

"But it doesn't unfix his alibi. I'd like to take this

register, sir. It will be returned as soon as possible. Sergeant Springer will write you a receipt for it. And I want a word with *you*," Montero added quietly to Ludlow.

They stood in the porch and looked with distaste at the heavy mist outside. Ludlow spoke of his curious encounter on the previous evening.

"You'll get yourself into real trouble one of these days," Montero said unsympathetically. "But thanks for the tip. I'll drop a word to the local superintendent about that bunch."

"I wonder," Ludlow said as if to himself. "There was a certain dignity – however. So you've solved the case, have you?"

"If we can break the biggest alibi you ever saw. Now look, this is important. Did you say anything to Finchley about that last entry in the diary?"

"Certainly not. I should think you ought to know by now that I am completely discreet. If it wasn't for my resourceful and courageous action in detaining him, you wouldn't have found Finchley yet. As for my being so foolish as to reveal matters which might assist him —"

"All right, all right, you didn't tell him. Well, just keep up being discreet, and I'll be obliged to you."

"Very well, Inspector. Since you counsel discretion, I won't trouble you with any further information."

"What does all that mean?"

"No, I'm being discreet. I can't say any more."

"For heaven's sake, what is it?"

"My lips are sealed, as a certain politician used to say. It's as well that you reminded me to be discreet. Otherwise I might have been tempted to tell you that at some unspecified time on the evening of the murder, Malving was seen near the church with a woman. My informant seemed to think that he was trying to evade observation. But now I shan't be so indiscreet as to say anything about it."

Ludlow walked off into the mist, leaving the inspector looking as if a host of new and troublesome ideas had settled in his mind.

CHAPTER ELEVEN

By Sunday the weather had become bitterly cold, but the threat of fog disappeared as if the new moon had cleared the air for presentation of its brief evening glory. The church was crowded for Evensong, the normally active parish congregation having been swollen by the seekers after sensation. The worshippers huddled into their pews as if to draw some hidden warmth from the varnished wood. The heating-system, after years of neglect through lack of money, was not functioning efficiently and a miasma of cold crept up through the iron gratings that should have uttered comforting warm air.

The churchwardens sat in central pews, one on each side of the aisle, their dignity of office marked by red cords that barred entrance to lesser mortals but now hung doubled back on brass hooks. The sockets which could hold their staves of office were empty, for this was no great festival, no episcopal visitation, but an ordinary Sunday towards the long end of the Trinity season. Plates were propped in front of them, ready for the collection. Cyril Blanch was comfortably rotund, fitting into his seat as if it had been carved out for him, and looking with mild academic interest as the service went on. Phillip Overley, more tense and alert, had the appearance of a greater involvement, a responsibility for all that happened in his presence.

Benjamin Farrow sat with his wife near the front of the nave. The hearty ex-soldier of a week ago had become an old man, worn and apologetic in his movements. Sarah White, despite her parish office, was right at the back behind a pillar. She looked as strained and unhappy as when Ludlow had seen her. Miss Mason, sitting upright like a fierce judge, shook her head and grimaced at frequent intervals as some point of ritual distressed her; she seemed like an ingenious clockwork toy, built to react to certain stimuli. Mrs. Acres, plump and sleepy, showed no sign of being aware of anything that was being done or said but turned a beaming face towards the chancel. Over all the regular members of the congregation there seemed to brood an air of defiance and militant rectitude, as if they were saying, "We are innocent. We know nothing about the dreadful thing that has happened, and here we are properly in church to prove it."

From the chancel steps Twotten gave out the notices, his hands shaking a little with the cold that hit him so cruelly after his years in Africa. He hurried through the announcements of services and meetings, then turned and bowed stiffly to where Malving was sitting with his hands clasped and his body bent forward like a man in pain. Malving got up, genuflected to the altar with an amplitude that brought some quite audible tutting from Miss Mason, and walked slowly to the pulpit.

"But the tongue can no man tame; it is an unruly evil, full of deadly poison." The congregation settled back in their places as Malving spoke his text, and prepared to listen to a few minutes of denunciation of sins which were committed only by other people. In spite of the cold, a restful air came over the church, the relaxation of people who believed that they were not being asked to do anything. Malving began hesitantly, but soon got into the full flow of his sermon. He spoke well and fluently, marred only by a tendency of his voice to trail up into a squeal when he got particularly emphatic. He dealt with questions of slander and scandal, saying nothing that was likely to cause any theological stir among the extremist members of the congregation on either side. After some fifteen minutes he hesitated, seeming to have ended, then leaned forward over the pulpit and began to talk rapidly in a more personal tone than previously.

"There are people in this parish, people in this very congregation, who have never learned the lesson of charity. Some of you have found in the tragic death of our beloved Vicar, not sorrow but only an opportunity for malice. The tongue is a wicked thing, an evil thing, when it is used to destroy a person's character. Some of you, sitting here at this moment, have been using it in just that way. You may think it is amusing to make charges and accusations without any cause. You may think it is harmless, mere passing gossip. I tell you that it is the Devil's work, and it must cease. If you could understand the misery caused by gossip —"

Malving broke off suddenly as if his voice would not obey him any more and bowed his head in a movement that might have been defiance or submission. He came rapidly down the steps from the pulpit, while Twotten announced the final hymn. The people groped in pockets and handbags while Blanch and Overley moved along to take the collection. The service was soon ended and the congregation streamed out with a flurry of feet and a deposit of hymn-books. There was no lingering in the porch, but people broke up and went their ways without speaking, driven perhaps by the cold night and perhaps by something more.

A stocky, neatly-dressed man with a fair moustache waited until the church was almost empty, then went up the side aisle and peered round the door into the vestry. In the ante-room, the choir were disrobing in silence unlike their usual cheerful chatter after the service. The man threaded his way through them and came to the vestry proper. The two clergymen were trying to avoid each other's eyes, a difficult and ostentatious task in that small space. With his back to both of them, Farrow was sitting at the desk counting the collection. From there he could see the door on his left, and he stiffened and stopped counting when the stranger came in. A hopeless look spread over his face.

"Forgive my butting in," Inspector Montero said

courteously. "I wondered whether Mr. Malving could spare me a few minutes. Is there anywhere private we could talk?"

In spite of Montero's protests that he wanted to disturb nobody, Twotten and Farrow both gathered up their things and went into the choir vestry, Twotten shutting the intervening door firmly behind him. Montero stood looking at Malving, apparently not so anxious to get on with his questions after all.

"That was a powerful sermon you gave us this evening," he said.

"I'm afraid I got rather carried away." Malving was as red-faced as a schoolboy. "I didn't mean to say so much, but there's a lot of beastly gossip about what happened – you know —"

"You mean that certain members of your flock think that they've found the murderer?"

"Well – people talk. Nobody believes anything really. Now I suppose they'll talk about my sermon. What does one do? If you speak platitudes, they say the Church is ineffective, but if you try to come home to them they say that we interfere in things that aren't our concern."

Malving spread his hands hopelessly and Montero smiled as if he understood. Without changing his expression except for a new keenness in his eyes, he spoke in a firmer tone.

"I was wondering whether you've had any ideas that might help me. Perhaps you remember something more about the evening when the Vicar was killed – someone you saw and spoke to around the church or while you were waiting at the Vicarage.

Malving shook his head. "I've told you all I know about that evening," he said. "There's nothing more."

"Well, never mind, it was just an idea. You've plenty of things on your mind as it is."

"What do you mean?" Malving spoke sharply.

"This worry about getting a house, for instance. I suppose all the negotiations are suspended while the parish is without a proper incumbent."

"Oh, yes, of course. I mean, there's nothing decided. Yes, it is rather worrying."

"It must be, both for you and for your fiancée. Is she a local girl, by the way?"

"No – she lives in Birmingham."

"That makes it more difficult, of course. Do you manage to see each other very often?"

"She's coming down next weekend, but that will be the first time for a month. We both have our jobs to do."

"Yes, indeed, and you've been hard at yours all day. I won't keep you any longer, but do let me know if you get any ideas. After all, who knows better than you what happens in this parish?"

Ignoring Farrow's frightened face and Twotten's inquisitive scrutiny, Montero went out through the choir vestry and walked down the empty church. Most of the lights had been put out, and only a faint glow showed up the bookstall just inside the main door, where a tall, lean figure was bent as if in serious study. Ludlow straightened up with suspicious haste when Montero approached The inspector merely nodded casually and walked past. Ludlow put down the book that he was holding and trotted indignantly after him.

"What did you think of the sermon?" Montero said after they had walked a little way down the road.

"Did you find out anything from Malving?" Ludlow asked.

"Now, who said that I'd spoken to Mr. Malving at all? You may be bursting with curiosity, but you really oughtn't to make it so obvious. It doesn't do for me to be seen running off and telling all my secrets to a civilian."

"I was only asking for information," Ludlow said sulkily.

"Like Rosa Dartle," said Montero, and the two men laughed with the relief of an allusion shared once again.

"Have you any rooted objection to drinking after church?" Montero asked.

"As one who thinks that many of the ills of our age can be traced to the rise of Puritanism, I see no reason for making a thing wrong at any particular time if it isn't wrong at others. Particularly as it's extremely cold, and the church was barely heated. I wonder why people in this country seem to find something devotional about being cold and uncomfortable. I have never been able to work out the puzzling equation of draught and religion."

"Like that church hall where you got yourself mixed up in a murder once before."

Montero shivered reminiscently, and the two men went into a pub which was casting a dingy light into the darkness. It was of the singularly dull kind which proliferates in parts of London, but it was warm inside. The two men sought a distant corner and sat down with their drinks. As was his custom with Ludlow, the inspector seemed to be thinking aloud rather than directly discussing the case.

"Malving isn't telling the whole truth," he said. "I'm sure of that, though whether what he's concealing has any bearing on the murder is another question altogether."

"Could his confusion be connected in any way with Sarah White?" Ludlow wondered.

"Sarah White. She's the secretary of the P.C.C. It's a thought, but I don't see anything to involve her. She didn't show much when we interviewed her, apart from a rooted objection to Miss Mason on theological grounds. Unless that business with Mrs. Acres and the flowers —"

"What's that?" Ludlow asked, too quickly.

"Never mind. It's a relief to hear you admit to not knowing something. What do you think of Sarah White, anyway?"

"I saw her for only a few seconds. She's quite a pretty woman, though obviously in a terrible state of nerves. She didn't look to me like a murderess."

"If they wore labels to distinguish them, our task

would be a lot easier. And once you think a woman is pretty she can get away with anything and still pull the wool over your eyes – I've seen it before."

"That is an uncalled-for and somewhat impertinent conclusion. But look here, a woman doesn't go and use a heavy service revolver."

"You'd be surprised what a determined woman can do. Anyway, what about some of the female resistance troops in the war? I agree that it's not the most feminine of weapons."

Montero waved his empty glass under Ludlow's nose and waited until it was refilled.

"What have you done about Finchley?" Ludlow asked when he had sat down again.

"We had to let him go, but we're keeping watch on him. So far he's given us no lead."

"I hope you realise that my resourcefulness and daring brought him into your hands."

"If you really want to know, I think he just used you as a tool to get himself picked up. The whole thing was just a bit too slick – evasive action and then eventually throwing himself in the way of an ingenuous don who happens to know how to use a telephone."

"Sometimes I wonder why I bother to help you at all," Ludlow said.

"Sometimes I wonder why I give you so much scope to interfere." Montero dropped his bantering tone suddenly and spoke seriously and in a quiet voice. "Look, Tom Finchley is all set up to have done it. But he's got an alibi that we just can't break. Twenty salesmen and an area manager have sworn independently that he was with them from just after seven until nearly ten on the night of the murder – and whatever you think of commercial travellers, you can't discount that sort of evidence. The Vicar was seen in the church well after seven, and the place where Finchley had this conference is on the other side of London."

"Finchley has a car, has he?"

"Yes, he gets one on the firm. Even so, he couldn't move backwards through time with it."

"He implied that he hadn't one, when he was so interested in getting transport home after you detained him."

"We spotted that. In fact he hadn't brought it out that evening, but it's typical of the sort of evasion he's been practising all the time; yet we can't shake his story."

"Perhaps some error of time, or of identity —"

"We coppers don't waste the taxpayers' money, you know. We've been into everything. Finchley was miles from here while the Vicar was sitting in the confessional, waiting for – well, who?"

"Whom. That's a secret that died with him. What more have you found out about Finchley?"

"He got a fair education and didn't do at all badly during the war. Since then, he's just drifted from one job to another, with periods of unemployment. He gambles a good deal, but more than that he hasn't the sort of temperament prepared to do steady work for someone else. In fact, he's the sort that becomes a crook — but there's no record and no trace of any criminal association. His uncle helped him out several times, but apparently was getting fed up. We don't know whether he ever told Finchley about what was coming to him in the will."

"Any family?" Ludlow asked.

"The Vicar seems to have been the only blood-relation living. Finchley married just after the war – a small-time actress of some kind. He says they separated and that he doesn't know where she is."

"Is there any possibility that he could be connected with these outbreaks of apparent Satanism in the church?"

"We can't get any sense at all out of that business. Funny to think that it's what brought us into this district in the first place."

They were silent for some time, until the lights were dimmed around them and the barman began collecting glasses and piling chairs on tables. They stood for a moment in the cold street.

"I wish you could get some bright idea about where those books are," Montero said. "They might lead us to the murderer or the Satanists – or both."

"I've already wasted a lot of time and paper over that question. I had the impression that Finchley was just as anxious as you over their whereabouts."

"Well, let me know if you think of anything. Want a lift?"

"Thank you, but no. A man in my profession has to be careful about being seen in bad company late at night."

With that final shot, Ludlow waved his hand and walked briskly away. However, as soon as Montero's car had passed him and gone out of sight, he turned and started walking back. Though the thought of his bed urged a strong counter-attraction, he was impelled by one of the unformulated guesses which had more than once brought him either credit or trouble in the past. If he could see the church at this hour, dark and empty, he might learn something that disappeared when there were other people helping to fulfil its normal function of worship. If this was more than an ordinary crime, if there were strange and evil forces behind the Vicar's death, the answer had to be sought in the peril of desolation. If not, any elimination would be useful.

The churchyard was not very large, and after the first fifty years it had been filled right up to its surrounding walls. In the cold darkness of a November night, it offered no elegiac sweetness, no setting for a pleasantly pastoral melancholy. Massive crosses and headstones of a Victorian pattern broke into the night with shapes of deeper blackness. The gate creaked as Ludlow pushed it open. His intention was to survey the church from all sides before seeing how difficult it might be to get inside when it was locked.

Stumbling on the uneven ground, he moved round the long wall on the south side. Overhanging trees at the corner made it impossible to see anything, and he felt his way round the building until his hand passed from stone to wood. This was the door out of the vestry, opening on to a gravel path towards the other and less-used gate out of the churchyard.

Ludlow shivered as a cold gust came and reminded him that it was some time since he had eaten and that the effects of the pub were wearing off. He decided to make a quick circuit of the church and then go home. As he moved forward again, his eyes now accustomed to the darkness, he suddenly realised that he was not alone in the churchyard. There were sounds of movement, slight but definite, and a faint sound that might have been a whisper if it was not indeed only the rising and falling of the autumn breeze. He took a few steps and then stopped, his heart beating quicker and with a very uncomfortable feeling in his stomach.

About ten yards away there was a particularly large and ornate tomb, with a flat stone raised some distance above the ground. Something was rising over the edge of the stone, dimly silhouetted against the dark sky, moving so slowly that it was hard to see whether it moved at all. But at last the flatness of the tombstone broke into an irregular shape that showed something perched on top. There was some semblance of the human form, but the body seemed to have no regular contours until it narrowed into what might have been a man's head if it were not topped by two branching horns.

The terror of the dark passage in the derelict house faded into oblivion. Although he tried to reassure himself that this was the very thing that might lead him to the heart of the mystery, Ludlow felt very unhappy and started calculating the distance to the gates. But to go one way was to turn his back on the thing squatting over the tomb, and the other would force him towards it. There was a rustling noise. Below the level of the stone, something was moving round and round.

A car rushed past in the road outside and its familiar sound brought Ludlow back to the twentieth century. Although he has often spoken scornfully of the cult of science, the realisation of being in a technical age gave Ludlow a courage that surprised him. He stepped resolutely forward, trying to feel sceptical and at the same time to remember some kind of useful exorcism.

His experience in the last search had taught him to bring a powerful torch, and he now drew it from his pocket and gripped it firmly. Whatever creatures awaited him, they seemed unaware of his advance. He was nearly there, and the thing on the stone was still mysterious, shapeless. Then he collided with something soft.

It was not Ludlow who screamed with terror at the encounter. When he switched on his torch, its light revealed two girls of about fifteen or sixteen, two very human and ordinary girls with too much make-up. As they realised that Ludlow was as human as themselves, they started to giggle.

The thing on the tombstone twisted away as Ludlow

threw the light in its direction. It had arms that tried ineffectively to hide its face. Ludlow sighed and cast up his eyes in despair. Draped in a sheet, with two horns of cardboard attached to his head, Cyril Blanch looked very foolish indeed as he clambered down to the ground.

CHAPTER TWELVE

"Don't tell the Senior Common Room about this," Cyril Blanch pleaded a few minutes later in the vestry.

His tawdry disguise was trailing across a corner of Farrow's desk on to the floor. Ludlow stood and regarded him severely, hoping that the shivering which the cold churchyard had begun in him would not be taken for any delayed symptom of fright. The bleak vestry seemed now like a haven of civilisation, an island of sanity where sacrilege and murder were banished by the solid, ugly furniture and strength of well-ordered records.

"It was two of the girls from the choir," Blanch explained feebly. "After there had been so much fuss about the traces of Satanism in the church, they got talking to me one day after the service and asked me what it was all about. I tried to explain to them about medieval witchcraft and all that sort of thing. It's not my subject of course, but you know how one likes to help — "

"I've never yet seen a member of our profession inhibited by ignorance from giving a long explanation of anything," Ludlow said. "But you really ought to know better than to embark on such subjects with adolescent girls. If you have read anything at all on the subject, you must know that various kinds of sexual promiscuity played a large part in these cults. Whether they began with morbid curiosity or not, I'm sure that these stupid girls ended with a large measure of it."

"How did you know about that?" Blanch murmured, looking very uncomfortable.

"Without sharing the pretensions to omniscience of some of our colleagues on the subject, I have a little knowledge of elementary psychology. He didn't know all the answers, but at least two cheers for Freud are sometimes in order. So you were then moved to give a practical demonstration."

"I said that I'd show them how the witches used to have their ceremonies. I was going to play the part of the devil, and they would pretend to be witches. It was just a game – we weren't going to do anything more than you saw. There wasn't anything wrong."

"But no doubt you were all hoping that there would be."

Ludlow's distaste was submerged in a swift flood of compassion, an imaginative sharing of the lonely world of fantasy, the mounting excitement, the fear that mingled with desire. He sighed and shook his head, not at having to witness the shame of a colleague but at all the inadequacy and deprivation that drove men into dark paths.

"There doesn't seem to have been any great harm

done," he said more gently. "But I must know one thing – did you have any part in the outbreaks that began all this trouble?"

"No, I swear I didn't. I wouldn't do anything like that – what you saw tonight was just a personal lapse. I try to serve this church and parish, and I want things cleared up as much as anyone. It was the worry that drove me to the sort of stupidity that's just happened."

"Worry about what?" Ludlow asked quickly.

"About the Vicar being murdered, of course. You know that the police have been suspecting me ever since we arrived together to find them at the Vicarage. And now there's this trouble about the will. I can't take any more. Ludlow, go away and tell them what you like but leave me in peace."

"What's wrong with the will? How does it concern you?"

"Miss Mason is trying to fight the legacy to the Guild of Saints Cyprian and Severus. That awful man Sprott is backing her up and offering funds to contest it in the courts. That means more publicity and trouble for the parish – after the murder, and the Satanism, and the affair of the Curate's house. And the churchwardens will have to be in the thick of it. I just don't know what I'm going to do."

"Ah, yes, I'd heard something of the sort. So she's really taking it seriously, is she? On what grounds is she contesting?"

"She says that the Vicar was mentally incapable when he made the will."

"Does she, indeed?" Ludlow looked very thoughtful. "I think you said something of the kind yourself on one occasion."

"I didn't mean it. He was a wonderful man really."

"One person didn't think so. However, Miss Mason's zeal can only do good to the parish to which you are so devoted. I imagine that if the courts set aside this particular bequest, it would be added to the residue of the estate which comes to the parish."

"She isn't doing it for that. She's just trying to make trouble, as usual."

"I wouldn't try to judge another person's motives, Blanch. In the present circumstances you may indeed be grateful for that forbearance."

Ludlow let himself out of the side door with the satisfaction of having a good exit-line. By the time he had stumbled across the churchyard and back to the main road, he was rebuking himself for a lack of charity which loved the epigram more than the individual.

On the following afternoon he found himself expiating this and other sins by drinking tea, which he dislikes, with Miss Mason, whom he was coming to dislike even more. Settled uncomfortably in the chair which Sprott had occupied, he looked with disapproval at the ghastly furnishings of the room, the heavy ornaments which stood up as stiff and minatory as their owner. Trying to win her confidence, if such a quality existed inside that leathery figure, he listened patiently to her recital of the wickedness that went on in the parish and which it was her appointed mission to combat.

"The late Vicar was liable to forgetfulness, I believe," Ludlow said when he could get in a word.

"He was mentally incompetent. At least, that's the only charitable explanation of some of his conduct. He was completely under the influence of men like Overley, who are trying to drag us all back to Rome. But a few of us are still not afraid to fight for the truth."

"I know that you are a fruitful worker in the Lord's vineyard, Miss Mason," Ludlow said. Feeling that he had not put it very well, he coughed and added hastily, "Have you any evidence that the Vicar was at all disturbed in his mind – the sort of evidence that would bear legal investigation?"

"Well, he was always forgetting things – appointments and so on. And now those books that he put somewhere and nobody can find. And he could never make up his mind about anything – look at the way he behaved about the parish house. Not that young Malving deserves any sympathy, because he's as near a papist as any of them. Let me tell you what he put into the service only two weeks after he came here — "

Ludlow sat back and let the story flow over him for a few minutes until he could see another opening.

"I doubt whether what you say about the Vicar would be accepted in court," he said eventually. "For instance, if there were any question of contesting his will —" He paused, anxious not to press too much and too soon, but Miss Mason was willing enough to talk.

"We shall certainly contest it, and we shall have it set aside. This parish may be full of iniquity, but better that the money should go here than to those people who call themselves the Guild of somebody or other. Oh yes, we shall contest it."

"We being yourself and —- ?"

"Mr. Sprott has promised the support of his society."

"I don't think I have the pleasure of knowing Mr. Sprott. He no doubt is another valiant defender of the truth?"

Ludlow started to put down his cup and take out his pipe, but decided that the pipe would be unwelcome and the cup in danger of being refilled. He sat and suffered the premonitions of indigestion while Miss Mason was eloquent about Sprott and the noble work of saving Britain from delusion and persecution that went on under his direction.

"Was Mr. Sprott acquainted with the late Vicar?" Ludlow asked when there was another chance.

"He was a thorn in his side." Miss Mason did not make it clear which of the two men played which role, and Ludlow did not press the question.

"The counsels of Mr. Sprott might have prevailed if the Vicar had not been cut off in his folly," Miss Mason went on. "He was with me here the very evening when the Vicar was struck down, and was planning to call on him yet again and try to make him see reason."

"Sprott was here that evening, was he?" Ludlow sat up and had to do some quick fielding to stop his cup and saucer going on the floor. "Did he in fact see the Vicar?"

"He decided to postpone his visit. It was late and he was tired after his good work of the day. He went into the church just before he came here, but said nothing about having seen the Vicar there."

"Did you go into the church yourself that evening? The time when the Vicar was there is very important."

"No, I didn't. I seldom go into the church except for the services on the Lord's Day. To attend worship in the church of my parish is a plain duty, but I can't pretend to get any edification from the scandalous irregularities permitted in the building itself. Anyway, the fact that he was having one of the popish pratices that he called confession made me particularly anxious to keep out on that evening."

"But Sprott was in the church." Ludlow mused deeply on this and forgot where he was until Miss Mason sharply recalled him.

"Mr. Ludlow," she said firmly, "perhaps you will now offer me some explanation of why you are asking all these questions. You asked if you could see me this afternoon, but the real purpose of your visit has not yet emerged. You are known to be a friend of Mr. Blanch —"

"No, just a colleague. Blanch has nothing to do —"

"And we all know what he and the other church-warden are like. I am beginning to fear that you are here to make mischief in the parish, or perhaps to hinder the work to which I have set my hand. Let me tell you that the judgement of the Lord will not be delayed. If you are trying to cover up the truth, there are those of us who will see that you shall not be able to do so for ever."

Ludlow got up, carefully and thankfully deposited his cup and saucer and looked at Miss Mason with sincerity.

"Let me assure you," he said, "that so far from wanting to cover up the truth, my only wish is to help to find it. If we can trace in detail the movements of the Vicar up to the time that he died, we shall be able to discover who killed him."

Miss Mason snorted like an indignant horse.

"There's no mystery about that," she said. "He was killed by his nephew, who stands to gain from the will. That legacy is another proof that the old man didn't know what he was doing and could be persuaded to anything. The police have been talking to him – it's been in the paper. You can leave that problem to them."

"The nephew has a strong alibi," Ludlow said gently.

"I dare say. A crowd of men will swear anything to save one of their friends from trouble. Personally, I don't believe a word of it. Men!"

Ludlow went downstairs with the feeling that he was being charged with all the male brutalities of history. But perhaps it was not only the wish to escape from Miss Mason that made him move more quickly than usual and look at his watch with such impatience. Was there time to follow up his ideas, or would it have to wait until the following day?

A hasty journey half across London was rewarded by finding that Mr. Sprott's office was still open. Unlike the Guild of Saints Cyprian and Severus, this society carried no visual images and held no trace of incense. The outer room was well stocked with tracts of an evangelical nature and decorated only with framed texts, each one bearing a discreet note of its price in the League's list. Ludlow did not have to wait long until Sprott himself came to welcome him into the private office.

Still wincing from a hearty handshake, Ludlow dropped into a chair and started to explain his interest in recent events. Sprott looked at him with curiosity and a kind of enormous patience that expected nothing but bad from most people but was prepared to put up with it.

"I know you weren't exactly a friend of the late Vicar," Ludlow said, "but I'm sure you would be the first to want his murderer detected."

"Poor man, poor man, sent to his account without time for preparation. It is a warning to us all, Mr. Ludlow. Long may we be spared to profit by it. However, justice must be done. I believe that the police are not unhopeful."

"There are still some points on which they have asked for my assistance," Ludlow said, lying so wildly that it was surprising the virtuous walls did not collapse around him. "I believe that you were in the church on the evening of the murder. May I ask at what time?"

"It must have been a few minutes before half past seven. I was to call on Miss Mason at the time, and I was a trifle early. I went into the church though I fear I cannot claim to have been greatly edified by what I saw. A sorry sight, Mr. Ludlow. Was it for this that our ancestors strove?"

"Did you see the Vicar?" Ludlow asked, side-stepping Sprott's last question.

"There was no sign of him. I think I was the only person in the church."

"And did you go straight from there to Miss Mason?"

"Indeed, yes. Her flat is very close to the church, you know. What a very good woman she is. Strong in the cause of truth, fearless in a very difficult situation. We should be hard put to it to get any response to our aims in that parish without her. But she is winning support and no longer fights quite alone. The time may be at hand when those who hold authority will stir themselves to cast down the altar of Baal; Judges, six, twenty-eight."

During this speech Ludlow had been trying to keep his face fixed in an expression of pious interest and was finding it a strain. At the last words he suddenly sat up and banged the table with his hand. Sprott looked at him in astonishment, turning to something like alarm.

"Have you got a Bible?" Ludlow asked.

"Why, of course. Would you like me to find a text for

us to discuss together? Is there any particular need which you feel at this moment?"

Sprott produced a large Bible. Ludlow grabbed it from him and started thumbing rapidly through it. In a few moments he gave a yell of triumph, leapt to his feet and rushed out of the office. Sprott was left with his mouth open and the Bible open on the table in front of him. He spent some time trying to discover what had made Ludlow so excited, but without success. He was still puzzling over it when Ludlow was scrambling out of a taxi in front of New Scotland Yard.

"It only makes the whole thing harder, unless we can do something with these times," Montero said.

With Springer assiduous in support as usual, he was worrying over the latest piece of evidence on the case. Door-to-door investigations near the Vicarage had yielded nothing; in those large houses, mostly divided into flats, people scarcely knew the names of those on the floor below and took not a bit of notice of comings and goings at the Vicarage. Now, however, one of the detectives had learned that a car had been seen driving away from the Vicarage very fast on the evening of the murder; skilful questions had at last brought the time to about a quarter to seven.

"Which doesn't get us far, even if it's right," Springer agreed. "The old man was alive a good time after that. Whoever it was, only the Vicar knew and he's dead.

Mrs. Acres had gone out long before that, so we're no further forward."

"It might have been the Unknown Penitent," Montero said. "We still don't know who it was who failed to turn up in the church that evening. Not that finding out would necessarily be any help, but I wish I knew. There's nothing more on Malving, is there?"

"He seems to be clean. If you'll allow me, sir, I reckon that we've got too many trails going on and we'd do better to follow one of them."

"Agreed, but which one? Finchley has every motive and opportunity but a perfect alibi. Farrow had motive, opportunity and means and no alibi, but there's no real evidence against him. Malving has been behaving in a peculiar way and may have had a grudge about his house, but one can hardly see him as a murderer. The fact that he's been seen in the dark with a woman while his fiancée's away may be morally regrettable, but it wouldn't impress a jury. Do we have to name any more?"

Before Springer could answer, the telephone on Montero's desk rang. Springer picked it up and in a few seconds his long face took on a look of mingled resignation and excitement.

"Mr. Ludlow's downstairs, sir," he said, covering the mouthpiece, "and yelling that he has to see you at once. Shall I go and calm him down – or tell him to get the hell out of it if you like?"

"Let him come up," Montero said. "He's not half as

clever as he thinks he is, but he does get through to the centre sometimes. Anyway, even a university don can't make this case more complicated than it is already. Besides, if he's got some crazy notion that means nothing, we could do with a good laugh."

A modified version of this message was sent down the telephone, and Ludlow was soon in the office.

"Have you got a Bible?" were his first words, received with less enthusiasm than Sprott had shown for them.

"You've come to the wrong place for the prayer-meeting, Mr. Ludlow," Springer said.

"Well, never mind. I think I have the text in my head."

"Now look here," Montero said wearily, "I appreciate that so much contact with the church may be affecting you, but I really haven't time for theological discussion."

"I do wish that a man of your intelligence wouldn't use 'appreciate' to mean 'understand'. Not that you do understand anything. I had it in mind to tell you where the Vicar's last purchase of books might be found, but I see that you are too busy and so I shan't trouble you any further."

"Sit down!" Montero said, in a voice that had caused many criminals to quail and which even Ludlow obeyed. "Have you got the books?"

"No, but I think I know where they are."

"Where?"

"You're sure you're really interested?"

"Oh, get on with it."

"You will recollect the entry in the diary which caused so much bewilderment. 'Books delivered. N.B. must make safe. Perhaps 1K69.' Now since the books were not readily to be found, the Vicar obviously did make them safe, as he put it, before he was killed, But where? We know that he was in the habit of putting things in odd places, and using even odder means of reminding himself of what he'd done. But this was a difficult one to solve, until one suddenly took the easiest way."

"I thought you were explaining, not making it more difficult," Montero said. "If this is the way you teach your students – oh all right, do it in your own time."

"That is precisely what I was doing when you interrupted me. I repeat, one had to take the easiest way. For where would a clergyman first turn his thoughts – a good, devoted clergyman as we know the Vicar to have been? From what source would he most readily draw his ideas? Clearly, from the Bible. Now if we read that strange message with that understanding, it presents no difficulty. We find an abbreviation, which any student of the Bible would use automatically —"

"First Book of Kings, chapter 6, verse 9," Montero shouted like an evangelical preacher announcing his text to an open-air meeting. "Jack, go and find a Bible."

"I don't reckon there's one anywhere in the Yard, sir," Springer said.

"There's no need to send your sergeant on such a

difficult errand," Ludlow said. "Having the advantage of a trained mind, and one accustomed to associate words in their context, I have remembered the verse. It reads as follows: 'So he built the house and finished it; and covered the house with beams and boards of cedar.' There you are."

Montero look unconvinced and Springer scratched his head and seemed to be having nostalgic memories of the old days in uniform when life was less complicated.

"We've been through the Vicarage from top to bottom," Montero said. "Wait a minute, though. You did the attic, didn't you?"

"Perkins was up there, sir," Springer replied. "He's usually pretty reliable."

"Well, he may have missed something this time. 'Covered the house with beams and boards' – that must refer to the roof."

"I'm not at all sure that it does, in the context," Ludlow said. "It probably refers to the whole of the outer covering. But the only place where a modern house is finished with beams and boards is in the roof, so your impression coincides with mine."

"That really makes my day," Montero said. "Come on, Jack. We're going back to the Vicarage and we're going to search every bit of space between the top floor and the roof until we find them. I suppose if I say you can't come, you'll twist your way in somehow," he added to Ludlow.

"I haven't the least intention of coming," Ludlow

said. "It's already late, and I have better things to do with my evenings than hang about talking to policemen."

"I'm delighted to hear it. Thanks for your help, anyway. It won't solve the murder, but at least we shall know whether those books were really valuable enough to be worth killing for; also if any of them are missing. Can you find your own way out?"

Montero and Springer disappeared quickly down the stairs, pulling on their raincoats as they went. Ludlow followed slowly, looking pleased and distinctly amused.

In the flat above his shop, Overley stood and stretched his arms in a gesture of appeal. He was alone except for the profusion of images and religious pictures which gave the room the appearance of oddity rather than devotion. No answer seemed to come from the painted faces or the plaster daubed with red for blood. The redness seemed to burn behind his eyes and fill his brain as he turned to and fro trying to pray. He needed words but they would not come, blocked by the thing which he knew he had to do.

CHAPTER THIRTEEN

Springer banged his head for the third time, and let out a stream of words highly unsuitable for even the roof-space of a vicarage. Montero straightened up without similar disaster and brushed some of the dust off his trousers. He moved cautiously around the water-tank, treading on the planks which offered perilous footways across the joists. Except for faint hisses and bubbles from the tank, the place was silent. They seemed cut off from the movement of current life, thrust back into a dead world of empty trunks and discarded lumber.

"Plenty of beams up here," said Springer, rubbing his head, "and boards too, for that matter. But I'm blowed if I can find any books."

Montero was tapping the chimney-stack that bulged out of one of the inner walls. Springer disentangled his feet from a broken umbrella and came over to him.

"The bricks are loose here," Montero said. "I wonder if he made a place inside. Not the way I'd choose to hide valuable books, but we'd better have a look at it. See if you can loosen one of them without bringing the whole place down."

Springer was spared any further labours by the voice of Mrs. Acres shouting incomprehensible words through the entrance to their dusty prison. Closer attention revealed that Sarah White was in the house and was very anxious to speak to them.

Neither of the detectives showed any reluctance to come down. They passed in a cloud of dust through the upper floors of the Vicarage, and had brushed and sneezed themselves into reasonably good order by the time they reached the room downstairs where Sarah White was waiting for them. Even Montero, long accustomed to signs of human misery and anxiety, was shocked at the change in her. Her naturally pale and serious face now looked as if she was carrying the sorrows of a whole generation. She was standing when they came in, trembling slightly through her whole body and holding herself upright with a determination to see her task accomplished at whatever cost to herself. Montero persuaded her to sit down, while Springer opened his notebook as unobtrusively as he could.

"I ought not to interrupt you in the middle of your work, but it suddenly seemed certain that what I knew couldn't be kept back any longer." Sarah White spoke awkwardly, as if learning the words as she used them, but her voice was firm.

"You should certainly tell us anything you know," Montero said encouragingly. "How did you know that we were here?"

"I didn't know. I mean, I came here to see Mrs. Acres,

and she told me that you were up in the roof, and suddenly it seemed like a sign that I should talk to you."

"I see. What did you come to see Mrs. Acres about – pressed flowers, perhaps?"

"Pressed flowers? Oh, those – but that was months ago, for my class. Why should it be important now?"

"Perhaps it isn't. I shan't know until you've told me all that's on your mind."

"Well, I did really intend to confide in Mrs. Acres, because I hoped she'd tell me what I ought to do. She's very sensible, you know, and of course she was very fond of the Vicar so there wouldn't be any harm in telling her. But then I thought that I ought to tell you after all. It's been worrying me for a long time, first about whether I ought to speak to the poor Vicar himself and then after he was killed, I just didn't know what to do. Because I didn't want to cause him any trouble or worry – he was such a good man."

"We don't doubt that, Miss White," Montero said gently. "Nothing that you tell me can possibly harm him now, and it may help to find who murdered him. Take your time and say it in your own way as it comes to you."

"Thank you. It was at the P.C.C. meeting that it started – the last one before the Vicar was killed – the one when there was all the fuss about the parish house and the newspapers and all that. I expect you know that the dear Vicar was very careless and absentminded, and he never could keep papers in the right place. Well, I was sitting next to him of course, taking notes for the minutes. After the meeting I gathered up all my papers but when I got home I found one that wasn't meant for me at all. The Vicar had given me a whole sheaf of things to be dealt with, and he must have included this letter among them by accident."

She stopped and seemed unable to go on. The distant sound of traffic through the big window seemed to urge them on to act quickly. Montero had an uncertain feeling that things were happening elsewhere to which he ought to be attending. He bent his mind to the immediate task.

"Was it a letter from the Vicar to someone else?" he asked.

"No. It was in an envelope addressed to him and had been posted and delivered in the ordinary way. But it was a funny sort of letter, because there was no address, or signature, or 'Dear Vicar', or anything like that. Just a message. Oh! Now you know, and I hoped that I could get round it somehow. It serves me right for trying to be dishonest."

"You mean that we now know that you read the letter. Very natural, Miss White. I suspect that most of us would. Anyway, it might have been something that he wanted you to deal with and you had to make certain."

"Yes, of course." Sarah White looked happier. "But when I saw what was in it, I just didn't know what to do."

"Was it something discreditable to the Vicar?"

"It was horrible. Whoever wrote it was demanding money from him and making all sorts of threats. They were mainly about things that he did in the church and the services, and referring to all those nasty acts of Parliament that allow people like Miss Mason to make trouble."

"You mean the various Acts for the regulation of public worship and so on. Yes, I believe they do cause heat in ecclesiastical circles but surely it's a long time since there was any effective prosecution under them. I thought that the Church of England carried its extremes pretty happily nowadays."

"Well, yes, but people can still make trouble with the Bishop and things like that. And then the letter went on to accuse the Vicar of other things that just couldn't be true."

"What sort of things?"

"I couldn't tell you, I really couldn't bear it. Dirty, horrible things."

"And threatening to make them public if he didn't pay up? Quite a familiar story to us, Miss White, and certainly not proving that he was guilty of anything at all. Have you got the letter now?"

"No. I kept it for a time but then I burnt it. I know I had no right to, but it was such a worry. I just couldn't make up my mind whether to give it back to the Vicar and own up that I'd read it and ask to help him in some way. It seemed like a duty to the parish to do something – either stop things like that happening or prove there was nothing in it. And then when he was killed, I was frightened in case I'd done anything criminal like destroying evidence."

"Did you recognise the handwriting on the letter?" Springer asked.

"It was typewritten."

"Where was it posted?"

"I'm sorry, I don't remember."

Springer sighed with heavy emphasis and Miss White sniffed apologetically and dabbed her eyes. Montero's eyes seemed to be watering too as if in sympathy, but he gave a hearty sneeze instead and showed that he had been troubled only by the remnants of dust from the roof. He blew his nose and then spoke with courtesy as if nothing was worrying him.

"So you never told the Vicar or anyone else that you had this letter?"

"Oh yes, I told Father Malving about it."

Both the detectives sat upright and looked excited. Miss White seemed surprised but not unpleased at causing such a reaction.

"It was on the very evening that the poor Vicar was killed," she went on. "I went into the church, and there was the Vicar sitting waiting to hear a confession, and it seemed impossible that he could have done any of those dreadful things or that anyone could have wanted to get him into trouble. Then I was going home, and I met Father Malving just in the next street. He'd been to the hospital and was just going to the church. We stood talking and suddenly I started telling him all about it. I made him promise not to say a word to any-one, but he said that he ought to speak to the Vicar about it and at last I agreed. So I told him that the Vicar had been in the church."

"And did Malving in fact speak to him then?" Montero asked, since she had faltered and gone silent again.

"He told me afterwards that the Vicar had gone by the time he arrived. He went up to the Vicarage and waited about here for quite a long time, but by then the poor old man must have been lying dead inside. Then he met Mr. Farrow, and then Mrs. Acres came – but you know all this."

"Yes, we know it all, Miss White. I may say that if you'd spoken earlier we might have been saved some false starts. And if you'd kept the letter, we might have been much nearer to finding the murderer."

"It was typewritten," Sarah White wailed protest-ingly.

"Typewriters can reveal their identity to an expert. Still, it's no good worrying about that. I'm glad you had the sense to speak up at last."

When Sarah White had gone after a few more incon-clusive questions, she left two very exasperated detec-tives behind her.

"It's marvellous," Springer said with disgust. "She destroys an important bit of evidence, gets suspicion thrown on the Curate, and goes round worrying herself sick about it but not saying anything. When we came in here, she looked as if she was going to confess to doing the whole job, black magic and all. Can you understand what makes people like that tick, sir?"

"Yes, I think I can. She's a woman with a strong conscience and moral sense, and she could be driven demented by a conflict that would mean nothing to the types that we have to deal with. You ought to know by now, Jack, that murder is the crime that generally brings you least into contact with the professional criminal."

"Are we going back in that ruddy loft?" Springer asked.

"I suppose so, though I'm beginning to think that Ludlow was wrong in his interpretation. I don't know that the pleasure of proving that he doesn't know everything is worth all that dust. He's probably home with his feet up, having a good laugh."

It was dark by the time Ludlow reached the church, having neither put his feet up nor laughed since leaving Scotland Yard. Two lights high up in the nave made economical provision for any late worshippers, and before the altar the red glow of the sanctuary-lamp was comforting in the gloom. The door creaked shut behind him as he groped his way round the bookstall and stood wondering whether to risk more light. He had no wish to attract attention to his search. Avoiding the central aisle, he moved cautiously across the back of the church and down one of the sides. After going a few yards he stopped and gave a quickly suppressed exclamation.

The wall here was plain and clear, free from memorial tablets or devotional pictures. Above it, the window was a black patch against the night outside. The whiteness of the wall was defaced with black paint: an obscene image and a few scrawled words of the deepest blasphemy.

Pushed back by alarm and driven on by curiosity, Ludlow found that his feet were in fact taking him farther along the aisle. Searching for one thing, he had evidently stumbled upon another. Whoever the desecrator might be, he was starting early tonight. Thus prepared, it was less of a shock to approach the altar and find that all its ornaments had been turned upside-down. The frontal was torn across in a ragged gap.

He continued to move, retracing his steps down the opposite side without finding any more traces of interference. The church was silent, throwing back the echo even of his light footsteps. Yet all the time he felt certain that he was not alone, that someone was watching everything he did. He found himself murmuring Coleridge's lines about the man on a lonely road who once looks behind him and dares not look again 'Because he knows a fearful fiend doth close behind him tread'. For once, he completely failed to find any comfort in a literary quotation.

At the back of the church, near the door by which he had entered, a short flight of stairs led up to the gallery that ran around three sides of the nave. When the church was built, there had been a certain social distinction between those who sat downstairs and those who were crowded on the gallery benches, but it was many years since the upper level had been regularly used. As Ludlow emerged from the stairs and looked down on the empty pews below, he felt again the certainty of being observed. It was an effort to turn his back on the lighted area and grope his way along in search of the next stage.

He squeezed his way past the organ that occupied part of the gallery, the only thing there that showed any sign of recent use. On the other side of it, just distinguishable in the faint light, were more steps built into the angle of the wall. As he moved towards them, Ludlow found himself close to the mirror which was fixed above the keyboard and allowed the organist to see what was happening at the other end of the church. At that moment it was showing no solemn procession, no ritual for the music to accompany. What Ludlow saw, coming out of the vestry and advancing along the central aisle, made him dive for the steps.

The way up was in fact little more than a broad ladder with a handrail. What had seemed the key to one mystery now became the possible route of escape from another. Ludlow pulled himself up to the top, where a sloping door closed access to the next level. It seemed certain that it would be locked, that he would be left suspended there until that which he had seen in the mirror was upon him, but in fact it creaked open when he pushed. He scrambled through, hauling his long body up with an agility which he would have refused to show for anything less than self-preservation. It dropped shut behind him and he was in darkness.

A frenzied striking of matches revealed a switch near to his hand. It put on an electric bulb, hanging nakedly on its flex and giving faint light to the vast space around. He was standing under the roof, above the plaster ceiling that was so ornate from below but here was only a wilderness of plain laths. The space was boarded along the edges, giving just room for one man to move, and a few planks ran across the joists towards the centre. There seemed to be no possible way of securing the door from the gallery.

Remembering his conversation with the organist about the state of the roof, Ludlow moved very carefully along the boards, bowing his head under the sloping tiles. There was no other exit in sight, either back into the church or to the open air. He stood still and tried to concentrate but his thoughts were flying to only one thing. Even in the small mirror, he had been able to see menace and evil in the figure that came out from the vestry. There was no way out, no possible weapon. Then the door creaked again and began to open.

Overley straightened himself and looked stern. He

was carrying the long churchwarden's staff with its brass head and seemed ready to discharge his duty as an officer of the parish.

"What are you doing up here?" he asked.

"Just having a look round." Ludlow's voice was high and strained as he tried to answer casually.

"This is my province, you know. I'm in charge of everything up here." Overley nodded vigorously as he spoke and he tapped his staff on the boards to emphasise his words.

"What are you doing with that thing?" Ludlow asked.

"This is my rod of correction." Overley lifted the staff and shook it menacingly. Ludlow backed away along the boards.

"Whom are you going to correct?" Ludlow was strictly correct in his grammar even in a moment of stress.

"Myself. Always myself."

"You've been responsible for all those acts of sacrilege in the church, haven't you?"

"Yes." Overley spoke soberly and without apparent shame.

"Why did you do it?"

"But I had to, of course." Overley looked as surprised and innocent as a child.

"They were an outrage to the place that you were supposed to protect. Didn't that ever occur to you?"

"Yes, they spoil the church, don't they? That's why

I did them. I have to do the things that hurt me most, and it hurts me when anyone spoils my house."

"You don't *have* to hurt yourself, do you?"

"Oh, but I do. I have to suffer all the time, for the sake of the rest of you. Because you all depend on me. Because, you see, I'm God."

Overley threw back his head and gave a howl of bitter anguish, then started to run forward along the boards, flailing his staff above his head. Ludlow pressed himself tightly against the slope of the roof and tried to find something to hold. Then there was a sharp crack as the brass head of the staff caught the electric bulb.

In the darkness, the sound of running feet stopped for a moment, then started again erratically. Overley was moaning and sighing, blundering wildly about under the roof. Ludlow tried to shout a warning, but no words would come. The tearing of plaster and lath seemed to be dragging down the whole church.

The dim light from the nave flooded like a beacon through the jagged hole in the middle of the ceiling.

As Ludlow tried to will the action back into his limbs, he realised that he had been gripping tightly something lodged behind one of the main beams. He cautiously drew it out and was not very surprised to find that it was a parcel of books loosely tied in brown paper.

CHAPTER FOURTEEN

"He always seemed as sane as the next man when I spoke to him," Montero said.

"That type of paranoia is often slow to reveal itself. For a long time it was relieved by an over-scrupulous attention to his religious duties, until the conflict became too great. The desire to hurt what is most loved can become irresistibly strong in an unbalanced mind." Ludlow had recovered his courage and was ready to give a lecture on any subject.

"Well, I wish you'd been as slick to see it coming as you are now to explain it."

With Springer in attendance, the two men were sitting in the vestry with the parcel of books open on the table. Overley's body had been removed and detectives were busy taking measurements and photographs while Twotten paced about wishing for the quiet life of the African jungle.

"And another thing," Montero went on, "what do you mean by sending us on a wild-goose chase in the Vicarage, when you knew all the time that the books were here?"

"In the first place," Ludlow said with dignity, "I

didn't send you anywhere. It was you who decided that you knew where to go, and who was I to arrogate to myself the grave peril of contradicting a police officer. Secondly, I didn't *know* that they were here. But the Biblical passage in question referred not to any private place but to the great Temple, so it seemed more than likely."

"Well, you've got them, anyway, so I suppose I ought to be pleased with you. But I'm not."

"I'm not very pleased with myself," Ludlow said unexpectedly.

"Oh come on, sir, you weren't to know that he was round the bend," said Springer.

"None of us knew," Montero agreed. "Poor chap, perhaps he's better out of it. Now, are these books as valuable as you thought they might be?"

"There was never any question of more than one of them being valuable," Ludlow reminded him. "This isn't the best moment for a thorough examination, but I should say that the Elizabethan printing is genuine and that we have in fact a second copy of an edition of which only one specimen was thought to be extant."

"Nice for Finchley – and nice for the parish too. Did Overley know that they were up there, do you think?"

"I'm pretty sure he didn't. Being disturbed in his latest outbreak gave him the final push. I'd have been in a nasty position if he hadn't chanced to hit the light."

"Serves you right for interfering. I'm glad you're all right, though," Montero added with real feeling.

"Do you think that Overley killed the Vicar?" Ludlow asked, obviously somewhat embarrassed.

"No, and neither do you. There wasn't any link between the Satanism and the murder after all. But someone was after the old man before he was murdered."

Montero briefly related all that Sarah White had told him. Ludlow looked pleased and not at all surprised.

"That is very satisfactory," he said.

"I don't see why, since we haven't got the letter to prove anything or trace who wrote it."

"Quite unimportant. What you have told me makes the last question in my mind easy to answer. You might as well go ahead and get a warrant or whatever form in triplicate and official jargon you need to make an arrest."

"Very kind of you to give permission. Is there anyone in particular that you'd like me to arrest?"

"Who's your own choice, Inspector?"

"Look here." Montero dropped his bantering tone and leaned forward towards Ludlow. "Tom Finchley knew about the last scrawled entry in the Vicar's diary – the one that led us to the register where Finchley's own birth is recorded. Nothing had been made public about that, so whoever knew about it had talked with the murderer himself. Finchley is in this, right up to the hilt. We've got to make him lead us to the man who did it."

"The murderer needn't have talked," Ludlow said in an abstracted sort of way.

"You mean that Finchley was there himself when it was written? Everything points to it, but his alibi's unshakeable."

"If the Vicar was dead before seven o'clock, Finchley's alibi is worthless. Am I right?"

"Of course. But it's no good. Too many people saw him in this very church later than seven."

"Did they? Ah well." Ludlow seemed to dismiss the subject. "Another thing, doesn't it seem odd that the last entry in the diary should have been allowed to remain there at all? I mean, if the murderer had stayed long enough to see the Vicar write it —"

"He'd have torn out the page and destroyed it. We're not quite moronic, you know. Since it pointed so clearly to Finchley, why did his accomplice leave it there? I don't know, unless Finchley's alibi was so certain that it didn't seem to matter how many clues led to him. Unless we can do something to shake a whole battery of witnesses, it doesn't matter at all."

"The witnesses are honest and respectable enough, but the alibi can be broken. Are you willing to take part in a little experiment? Or perhaps a little amateur acting would be more appropriate. In fact yes, I think it would be a better description. After all, there's been a good deal of acting in this case, and not all so amateur either."

"Oh, for heaven's sake, man —" Montero began.

"Listen carefully before you decide," said Ludlow. He

settled back in his chair and started to talk as if the two detectives were students eager for instruction.

Ludlow's flat was looking so much less untidy than usual that anyone who knew him well would have known that he was expecting a visitor. It is true that most of the floor was still covered with books and papers, while the proofs of his latest article dangled perilously from the shelf above the electric fire, but he had managed to clear two chairs and to push the laundry parcels into the bedroom. A selection of drinks stood on a tray which had been wiped clean of all but its most stubborn stains. Ludlow had combed his hair and reluctantly exchanged his oldest sports coat for one which had fewer holes and still maintained a button or two. The fact that he was wearing odd socks was unknown to him and would in any case not have bothered him. Any of his students who had been looking through the keyhole would probably have gone away to spread the news that old Ludlow was getting ready to chat up a bird.

When the doorbell rang, Ludlow nodded with satisfaction but did not show any further emotion. He went and admitted his visitor, who walked straight in without speaking, threw down his coat and stood in the middle of the room looking aggressive. Tom Finchley's usual shifty, ingratiating manner had been replaced by hostility and suspicion. He was obviously bursting to ask some particular questions, but Ludlow appeared not to notice anything of the kind and simply pressed him to sit down and have a drink.

"This is rather an interesting one. The edition itself is of no great value, but if you look at the inscription on the flyleaf– "

Ten minutes later, Ludlow was deep in his favourite subject. He was producing some of the treasures from his small library and explaining in detail how he had come across them. Finchley had passed the stage of making polite noises and was sitting with a neglected glass in his hand opening and shutting his mouth at intervals while Ludlow rattled on.

"I seem to remember that you're interested in Elizabethan printing," Ludlow continued. "It's beyond the reach of us, unfortunately, but have you seen the reproductions made by some scientific process or other? The technicalities are beyond me, but the effect is remarkable. There are indeed moments when I think that science may not be an unmixed curse —"

"Stop playing." Finchley snapped viciously, putting down his glass. His weak face looked dangerous, with the savagery of a man pushed further into evil than he meant to go.

"I'm afraid I don't follow you," Ludlow said blandly.

"You follow all right. Why did you send for me?"

"Send for you? I really don't know what you mean. How could I venture to suggest that I was in a position to send for you? I'm glad you were able to come in for a chat and a drink as I suggested. We seem to have been so unfortunate in our previous attempts to talk about old books – something always happens to cut us short."

"Look here, Ludlow, I don't know exactly what you're up to, but I take it that you want to do a deal. I went to the Vicarage after I got your message. Mrs. Acres told me what had happened in the church. You've found the old man's books, haven't you?"

"Well, yes, I did come upon them. A pity about poor Overley —"

"We might as well come clean with each other. You and Overley knew what those books were worth, and you were going to carve up the profit between you. You shoved him through the ceiling so that you'd get the lot for yourself, but the coppers walked in before you had time to get the books away. You've managed to persuade your pal the inspector – or maybe he's in the deal too. But you're forgetting one thing – those books are mine. What have you done with them?"

"Inspector Montero has taken them away." Ludlow spoke as if answering a reasonable question from a student and ignored the rest of what Finchley had said. Finchley got up and clenched his fists.

"I want those books," he said.

"Then you'd better go to Scotland Yard. Anyway, only half the value is yours."

"I've a legal right to them. I'm going to see a solicitor."

"Now that's a very good idea, Mr. Finchley. It's liable to be an expensive business, but it's worth getting a good one. Yes, I really think that it's the best thing you could do."

"What's all that supposed to mean?"

"You can't get your defence arranged too soon. No doubt you'll be given every facility when you're in prison awaiting trial, but it will be so much more convenient to do it while you're still free."

Finchley took a step forward, then gave a sharp laugh and sat down again. He picked up his empty glass and held it to be refilled. Ludlow poured a small amount into it, and a large amount into his own.

"So that's your game, is it?" Finchley said. "You want to get me out of the way by making out that I killed my uncle, so that you can have a free run with the books. Maybe you've got your eye on his other things too. Well, it's just not going to work. The coppers have been trying to pin it on me ever since it happened, but no joy. I've got a lovely alibi, and you know it. Not even one of you blasted professors is going to break it."

"Let's try, shall we?" Ludlow said, settling himself comfortably. "I believe that impeccable witnesses have sworn to your being some miles away from the scene of the murder after seven o'clock. But what about the earlier part of the evening – say between six and seven?"

"You tell me what."

"Very well. You drove to the Vicarage about twenty to seven. From one of your little chats with Mrs. Acres, or perhaps from long observation, you knew that your uncle would be alone at that time and that he would cheerfully admit anyone who came to the door. He was probably not particularly glad to see you, but you were able to talk your way into the house and into his study. There you shot him, while he was at his desk getting out some money in fulfilment of your latest demand. Secure in the abibi that you had prepared, you then scrawled a few words on his open diary. The message was intended to point to you, and since you thought that you could never be convicted you hoped to stop any further investigations that might reveal any confederate who may have helped you."

"Just a minute. What about the gun? It was Farrow's gun that shot the old man, and it was kept in the church. Have you got a single witness to say that I was ever in the place?"

"I was coming to that. Let us again postulate the existence of a confederate, one who was frequently in and out of the church and whose presence there would cause no comment. That person could have procured the gun and handed it to you at some agreed point on your way to the Vicarage. A similar arrangement would have sufficed on the way back – a momentary pause on a dark stretch of road, and then you were away and driving hard to get to your meeting."

"Quick work." Finchley seemed greatly amused by all that Ludlow had said. He held out his glass again, but it was ignored.

"It was certainly quick work," Ludlow agreed, "but it was well planned. So well, in fact, that I detect the presence of a better brain than yours behind the planning. The direct route from the Vicarage to your meeting could easily be covered in fifteen minutes at that time in the evening. You were there by seven, no doubt feeling that you had succeeded. Your enthusiasm for the proceedings was exemplary and brought you to everyone's notice. You left three hours later, a jolly good chap to your colleagues and a promising salesman to the management."

"It's a lovely story. The only thing wrong with it is that even the police know that my uncle was alive well after seven."

"They have believed he was. Much to my regret, because I have a respect for the police, I have to declare them wrong."

Finchley looked uneasy for the first time but said nothing. Ludlow seemed to be listening as if expecting another ring at the door. He spoke more quickly, never taking his eyes off his visitor.

"The Vicar was never seen alive after Mrs. Acres left for the cinema – except by the man who killed him."

"A lot of people saw him in the church. Are you going to call them all liars?"

"Certainly not. Let us consider the possibility of being sincerely mistaken, before we call anyone a liar. What about optical illusions? A man may be convinced that two identical squares are of different sizes, because the effect of deliberate shading distorts his view. But are we to say that he is a liar? A number of worthy people *thought* that they saw your uncle in the church. People are easily convinced by familiar tokens externally. They seldom try to find the inner reality unless something is missing or out of place. If it had not been for one false note in the harmony, even I might have been deceived."

"Get on with your fairy story." Finchley sneered but he was pale and tapped the arms of the chair as he spoke.

"I have already postulated the existence of a confederate who both gave and received back the gun. Now suppose that person had immediately gone into the church, replaced the gun in the vestry, and then set out to create an optical illusion."

It had started to rain and a sudden flurry against the window seemed perfectly timed for the long pause that Ludlow made. Finchley's hands were still now, and his whole body was rigid with attention.

"In his daily relationships," Ludlow went on, "a priest is a man like the rest of us – a known, recognisable individual. But when he is performing his sacred duties, he becomes a figure of ritual; he assumes a different and impersonal aspect. We identify him by what he wears and what he does, rather than what he is. So if those who were in the church that evening had seen someone sitting in the confessional, wearing the customary vestments, they would naturally have taken it to be the Vicar. The size and general outline of the figure made sure that it was not Malving, and who else could it be?"

"I can't wait to hear." Finchley's voice was hoarse.

"It was in fact your associate or confederate, who put on the cassock, biretta and other vestments, and then went and sat in the one position where it was certain that no one would come and try to talk. It was not a regular time for confessions. If the Vicar was waiting for a special penitent, people would not approach him, would not stare in his direction. So the illusion was kept up for long enough, until the impersonator could go out slowly, imitating the Vicar's walk, remove the vestments and slip out by the side door from the vestry."

Finchley half rose, then dropped back into his chair. With an obvious effort he laughed, but both his hands were shaking as he took out a cigarette.

"It's a nice story. Now prove it," he said.

"Certainly, if you wish. I have said that no one would look closely at a priest on such an occasion. However, there was one person in the church who did not feel the usual restraint – an old man who often takes shelter there and amuses himself by watching what is going on. He told me something very interesting. The person whom everyone took to be the Vicar was wearing a green stole round the neck."

"So what?"

"So it wasn't the Vicar. The colour for confessions is purple or violet. The green vestments were proper for the season and were of course in use for the ordinary services. Anyone not well-versed in liturgical colours would have picked up the one seen most recently, and which came easily to hand. But no priest would prepare to hear a confession in a green stole – and the late Vicar was known to be particularly traditional and correct in his practice."

"It's still only the word of an old man. You can't prove anything."

"Oh, but I can. Your wife has been very co-operative and has told me all I needed to know. When she was confronted with the mistake about the colour of the stole, she admitted that it was she who had impersonated the Vicar in order to give you an alibi. She nearly got away with it too —"

The doorbell was like an alarm, cutting them both off in the middle of their reactions. Finchley leapt up, fury and terror mingled in his face. Ludlow stopped talking and walked away into the little hall, carefully shutting the door from the main room. His voice could still be heard, however, as he opened the front door.

"Good evening, Miss Mason. It's extremely good of you to come, and I'm only sorry that it's turned out to be such wretched weather. Let me have your coat. Now come in, and we can talk more comfortably. As I said on the telephone, I am very anxious to discuss the question of the Vicar's bequest to that society —"

Ludlow was still talking as he ushered her in. Miss Mason and Finchley stared at each other, incredulity turning slowly to anger.

"You bloody bitch," Finchley said. "So you've squealed, have you? He's just been telling me about it."

He grabbed the decanter from which Ludlow had been dispensing whisky and rushed at her. Miss Mason struck out with her grim leather handbag and knocked the weapon from his hand. Finchley swung his fist, but the arm behind it suddenly stopped in mid-air and he was dragged roughly backwards.

"All right, break it up," said Sergeant Springer.

Montero emerged from the bedroom after him, not seeming to be in any particular hurry. Before he could begin the caution and charge that were on his lips, Finchley had torn himself free and bolted out of the door. Ludlow looked questioningly at the two detectives and made tentative movements without any real enthusiasm.

"There's a man by the lift and another on the stairs, as well as one on each of the exits below," Montero explained. "He won't get far."

"What is the meaning of this outrage?" Miss Mason demanded. "I had no sooner entered the room than I was set upon."

"We'll take you too, Mrs. Finchley. Come along," Montero said.

Ludlow picked up the fallen decanter and examined it carefully, after making a feeble attempt to mop up the whisky with his handkerchief.

"I believe that it's cracked," he said. "I intend to claim compensation from the Home Secretary, or whoever deals with these things."

CHAPTER FIFTEEN

"It was when you said that Finchley had married an actress that the idea first came to me," Ludlow said.

He was sitting in Montero's office, making a long and rambling statement that was straining even Springer's skill in taking notes. As he reached the climax of his story, however, he stuck to the main point. The autumn had flickered out into dead winter; a chilly slime seemed to cover the outside of the great building and spread slowly down to the Embankment and the river below.

"It was obvious that everything pointed to Finchley's guilt. He had quarrelled with his uncle, but through the old man's forgiving nature he stood to gain a substantial amount from the will. Not a fortune, but a temptation to a man who had made no success of life. Then came the possibility of one of the recently purchased books being a real treasure."

"Even we realised all that," Montero said with mock humility.

"Good. Now Finchley did all he could to draw attention to himself after the murder, starting with the false entry in the diary. He came to see me, drawn partly by genuine curiosity about the books and partly by the knowledge that you would soon learn about his visit."

"He had you fooled there, anyway. You thought you were leading him into a trap, when all the time it was exactly as he wanted."

"I knew what I was doing." Ludlow looked confused and coughed, while Springer ventured a sly wink at his superior. "However, as you say, it was exactly as he wanted. He wanted to be found, in circumstances that made things look suspicious, and then he made slips and told lies in his interrogation. He was so confident that his alibi could not be broken that he wanted to concentrate all your attention on himself and away from the manner in which things had actually been done."

"If it hadn't been for her mistake with the colour of the stole, she might have got away with it," Montero said.

"It would have been hard to prove, certainly, though I was already suspicious. You will remember that I had time to study the Vicar's diary on the night of the murder —"

"Interfering with evidence again," Montero said with a grin.

"You are the most ungrateful man I have ever met. Apart from the interesting things that I found in the diary, there was one equally interesting omission. The Vicar, notoriously forgetful and needing to write down every appointment, had made no mention of hearing a confession at that unusual hour. It was not conclusive, but it was certainly strange. Now what follows is largely conjectural, but it is a hypothesis that seems to fit the facts. Miss Mason, as we may continue conveniently to call her —"

"Let me fill you in on what we know. If I tell it, we shall all be saved a lot of time."

"I think that I detect an innuendo there, Inspector."

"Well, have it for a present. Mrs. Finchley, *alias* Miss Mason, has been singing to us like a bird. So your little lie to Finchley has been put right in retrospect. The two of them had been working a racket on the poor old Vicar. They'd never broken up as Finchley suggested, but they'd certainly had trouble in keeping things going. So when she found out that he had an uncle who was both rich and kindly, she made up her mind to get all she could out of him. The first thing was to find out his weaknesses, so she settled herself in the parish under an assumed name. She started persecuting him in all sorts of little ways, threatening him with litigation about various details that nobody worries over much today. At the same time, Finchley was also trying to wear him down, calling on him and also sending letters accusing him of things of which he was quite innocent."

"Yes, I guessed that she was the moving spirit," Ludlow said thoughtfully. "Of course, the Vicar had never seen her and she also had the advantage of being an experienced actress, even if not a highly successful one. Her aim was to bring herself into prominence in the parish as quickly as possible. Since the majority supported the Vicar in his high practices and ritual, the obvious course was to stand as a champion of the evangelical or Low Church cause. I need hardly say that she herself has no respect for any kind of churchmanship at all. But she was able to rally to herself the small section of the parish who disliked the Vicar's ways, and it was not long before she got herself elected to the Parochial Church Council. You agree with my analysis?"

"It's what she told us, though not quite in your terms. Anyway, the two of them were beginning to put real pressure on the old man – as witness the letter which Sarah White found. They hoped to soak him of a good deal of money at the price of her getting out of the parish and their both leaving him alone. It might have worked and it might not. But then the Vicar himself said something that virtually signed his own death warrant. He let out that he was leaving Finchley a substantial sum in his will. It was at the end of a P.C.C. meeting, and the woman he knew as Miss Mason was standing by. To him, she was a misguided but sincere woman; he didn't know that she was his nephew's wife and also a vicious type."

"So she thought that they'd get more by killing than by waiting," Ludlow said.

"Exactly. The apparent Satanism in the church gave cover for violence, and the criminal folly of Farrow putting a loaded gun in the vestry made it just too easy. She got hold of it, passed it to Finchley and then slipped it back into the drawer when she went to put on her little act. We didn't learn about the existence of that gun until next morning, you remember, and by that time it was back with one bullet missing – and a nice lead towards Farrow just to give more confusion. Is there anything else you want to know?"

"I had all that worked out, of course." Ludlow was not pleased to be kept silent for so long. "She replaced the revolver, vested herself as the Vicar with a complete disguise in the long cassock and the biretta to hide her hair, went and sat for long enough to create the illusion, then got home in time to receive Sprott as arranged. The poor man would have drunk his coffee with less enthusiasm if he had known what kind of woman she really was. Now, is there anything else that *you* want to know?"

"Yes. When you thought that someone had impersonated the Vicar, what made you suspect Miss Mason?"

"Ah, there I had the advantage of you. During a conversation with her, she showed herself strangely anxious to throw guilt on to Finchley. When I pointed out that he had an alibi, she said, 'A crowd of men will swear anything to save one of their friends from trouble.' Now you, with your usual discretion, had not made a public announcement of the nature of Finchley's alibi. How could she have known that he claimed to have been with a crowd of men who knew him?"

Montero pulled at his moustache, while Springer sucked his pencil and looked even more melancholy than usual. Happy at having received the attention due to him, Ludlow sat back and let them think about it.

"Fair enough, now that we've got the whole story, but hardly enough by itself," Montero said at last.

"Perhaps not, but a useful pointer. And our knowledge of all subjects is surely built up by following the right pointer, by associating apparent trivialities into an ultimate synthesis. Let me give you an example from the field of linguistics – you're not in a hurry are you?" Ludlow asked as both men looked at their watches.

"We've only got about a dozen other crimes to look into. But perhaps we could hear the rest of your fascinating lecture another time."

"She also said that she has particularly avoided going into the church on that evening, since the Vicar was indulging in what she regarded as the Popish practice of confession. But it was not one of his usual times, and everyone assumed that it was something special. No one could possibly have expected it – except the person who pretended to be the Vicar."

They were all silent again. The distant rumble of traffic crept up from the road far below. A telephone rang in the next room and was quickly answered. A door slammed along the corridor. Montero went and stood by the window, looking out over the city that he was committed to protect from crime as far as he could.

"Well, that seems to be about it," he said. "You certainly kept yourself alert. When we went over to that place first, we weren't looking for a murder. As it turned out, we uncovered a good deal more than a few amateur witches."

Ludlow nodded agreement, seeing Overley's twisted body on the tiled floor, with the gaping hole above. Then he remembered Blanch, ludicrous and pitiful in his disguise but there was no need to speak of that.

"What about Farrow?" he asked.

"I've handed his case over. He'll probably go down for embezzlement. And of course there's the firearms offence if they choose to proceed on it."

Ludlow got up and started collecting his scattered belongings from different parts of the office.

"Come round and have some more curry one evening," he said.

"Thanks, but this case has rather taken it out of me. I'll have to get a holiday and build up my strength before I can face any more of your cooking!"

Ludlow found himself drawn back to the church. Like a man who has suffered new and unhappy experiences in a place and needs to go back of his own accord to exorcise the memory, he walked slowly along the road that led to it. The building was drably grey in the late afternoon of fading December light, but the fussy details of architecture were obscured and the silhouette was plain and almost noble against the sky. The door still creaked when he pushed it open and went into the gloom of painted windows and incense-laden air.

The hole in the middle of the ceiling had been roughly covered with canvas until it could be repaired. Ludlow shivered as he looked up at the dark patch above the hanging electric lights and remembered the moment of terror under the bare roof. He sat down in one of the pews and let the faces of the recent past wreathe their shapes before his eyes until they sank into forgetfulness. He felt peace steal over him, an assurance that there was still a pattern of truth and reason, in spite of all that men did to break it. The church that seemed to draw out so many weaknesses and frustrations in those who professed to love it, that seemed to be condemned by their faults, was still there in the end to receive them back and set them right. Not once but time after time, there was reconciliation. And what men like the Vicar could do in their little way continued to be done. Unless life was a hollow joke, a mistake of cosmic chemistry, such things had to end in something more glorious than an old man's blood pouring out on a shabby carpet.

Ludlow got up and walked back into time. He went quickly away through the gathering dusk, crossing and cutting through the streets until nothing of the church was visible except the cross on the squat steeple. At the tube station he looked back and saw it still above the television aerials and the chimneys of terraced houses. The evening newspapers were proclaiming many woes, and the shops that sold tawdry things were decked with glittering colour for the season that they chose to call Christmas.

THE PERENNIAL LIBRARY MYSTERY SERIES

Ted Allbeury

THE OTHER SIDE OF SILENCE	P 669, $2.84
PALOMINO BLONDE	P 670, $2.84
SNOWBALL	P 671, $2.84

Delano Ames

CORPSE DIPLOMATIQUE	P 637, $2.84
FOR OLD CRIME'S SAKE	P 629, $2.84
MURDER, MAESTRO, PLEASE	P 630, $2.84
SHE SHALL HAVE MURDER	P 638, $2.84

E. C. Bentley

TRENT'S LAST CASE	P 440, $2.50
TRENT'S OWN CASE	P 516, $2.25

Andrew Bergman

THE BIG KISS-OFF OF 1944	P 673, $2.84
HOLLYWOOD AND LEVINE	P 674, $2.84

Gavin Black

A DRAGON FOR CHRISTMAS	P 473, $1.95
THE EYES AROUND ME	P 485, $1.95
YOU WANT TO DIE, JOHNNY?	P 472, $1.95

Nicholas Blake

THE CORPSE IN THE SNOWMAN	P 427, $1.95
END OF CHAPTER	P 397, $1.95
HEAD OF A TRAVELER	P 398, $2.25
MINUTE FOR MURDER	P 419, $1.95
THE MORNING AFTER DEATH	P 520, $1.95
A PENKNIFE IN MY HEART	P 521, $2.25

THE PRIVATE WOUND	P 531, $2.25
A QUESTION OF PROOF	P 494, $1.95
THE SAD VARIETY	P 495, $2.25
THERE'S TROUBLE BREWING	P 569, $3.37
THOU SHELL OF DEATH	P 428, $1.95
THE WIDOW'S CRUISE	P 399, $2.25

Oliver Bleeck

THE BRASS GO-BETWEEN	P 645, $2.84
THE PROCANE CHRONICLE	P 647, $2.84
PROTOCOL FOR A KIDNAPPING	P 646, $2.84

John & Emery Bonett

A BANNER FOR PEGASUS	P 554, $2.40
DEAD LION	P 563, $2.40
THE SOUND OF MURDER	P 642, $2.84

Christianna Brand

| GREEN FOR DANGER | P 551, $2.50 |
| TOUR DE FORCE | P 572, $2.40 |

James Byrom

| OR BE HE DEAD | P 585, $2.84 |

Henry Calvin

| IT'S DIFFERENT ABROAD | P 640, $2.84 |

Marjorie Carleton

| VANISHED | P 559, $2.40 |

George Harmon Coxe

| MURDER WITH PICTURES | P 527, $2.25 |

Edmund Crispin

| BURIED FOR PLEASURE | P 506, $2.50 |

Lionel Davidson

THE MENORAH MEN	P 592, $2.84
NIGHT OF WENCESLAS	P 595, $2.84
THE ROSE OF TIBET	P 593, $2.84

D. M. Devine

MY BROTHER'S KILLER	P 558, $2.40

Kenneth Fearing

THE BIG CLOCK	P 500, $1.95

Andrew Garve

THE ASHES OF LODA	P 430, $1.50
THE CUCKOO LINE AFFAIR	P 451, $1.95
A HERO FOR LEANDA	P 429, $1.50
MURDER THROUGH THE LOOKING GLASS	P 449, $1.95
NO TEARS FOR HILDA	P 441, $1.95
THE RIDDLE OF SAMSON	P 450, $1.95

Michael Gilbert

BLOOD AND JUDGMENT	P 446, $1.95
THE BODY OF A GIRL	P 459, $1.95
FEAR TO TREAD	P 458, $1.95

Joe Gores

HAMMETT	P 631, $2.84

C. W. Grafton

BEYOND A REASONABLE DOUBT	P 519, $1.95
THE RAT BEGAN TO GNAW THE ROPE	P 639, $2.84

Edward Grierson

THE SECOND MAN	P 528, $2.25

Bruce Hamilton

| TOO MUCH OF WATER | P 635, $2.84 |

Cyril Hare

DEATH IS NO SPORTSMAN	P 555, $2.40
DEATH WALKS THE WOODS	P 556, $2.40
AN ENGLISH MURDER	P 455, $2.50
SUICIDE EXCEPTED	P 636, $2.84
TENANT FOR DEATH	P 570, $2.84
TRAGEDY AT LAW	P 522, $2.25
UNTIMELY DEATH	P 514, $2.25
THE WIND BLOWS DEATH	P 589, $2.84
WITH A BARE BODKIN	P 523, $2.25

Robert Harling

| THE ENORMOUS SHADOW | P 545, $2.50 |

Matthew Head

THE CABINDA AFFAIR	P 541, $2.25
THE CONGO VENUS	P 597, $2.84
MURDER AT THE FLEA CLUB	P 542, $2.50

M. V. Heberden

| ENGAGED TO MURDER | P 533, $2.25 |

James Hilton

| WAS IT MURDER? | P 501, $1.95 |

S. B. Hough

| DEAR DAUGHTER DEAD | P 661, $2.84 |
| SWEET SISTER SEDUCED | P 662, $2.84 |

P. M. Hubbard

| HIGH TIDE | P 571, $2.40 |

Elspeth Huxley

THE AFRICAN POISON MURDERS — P 540, $2.25
MURDER ON SAFARI — P 587, $2.84

Francis Iles

BEFORE THE FACT — P 517, $2.50
MALICE AFORETHOUGHT — P 532, $1.95

Michael Innes

APPLEBY ON ARARAT — P 648, $2.84
APPLEBY'S END — P 649, $2.84
THE CASE OF THE JOURNEYING BOY — P 632, $3.12
DEATH ON A QUIET DAY — P 677, $2.84
DEATH BY WATER — P 574, $2.40
HARE SITTING UP — P 590, $2.84
THE LONG FAREWELL — P 575, $2.40
THE MAN FROM THE SEA — P 591, $2.84
ONE MAN SHOW — P 672, $2.84
THE SECRET VANGUARD — P 584, $2.84
THE WEIGHT OF THE EVIDENCE — P 633, $2.84

Mary Kelly

THE SPOILT KILL — P 565, $2.40

Lange Lewis

THE BIRTHDAY MURDER — P 518, $1.95

Allan MacKinnon

HOUSE OF DARKNESS — P 582, $2.84

Frank Parrish

FIRE IN THE BARLEY — P 651, $2.84
SNARE IN THE DARK — P 650, $2.84
STING OF THE HONEYBEE — P 652, $2.84

Austin Ripley

MINUTE MYSTERIES   P 387, $2.50

Thomas Sterling

THE EVIL OF THE DAY   P 529, $2.50

Julian Symons

THE BELTING INHERITANCE   P 468, $1.95

BOGUE'S FORTUNE   P 481, $1.95

THE COLOR OF MURDER   P 461, $1.95

Dorothy Stockbridge Tillet
(John Stephen Strange)

THE MAN WHO KILLED FORTESCUE   P 536, $2.25

Simon Troy

THE ROAD TO RHUINE   P 583, $2.84

SWIFT TO ITS CLOSE   P 546, $2.40

Henry Wade

THE DUKE OF YORK'S STEPS   P 588, $2.84

A DYING FALL   P 543, $2.50

THE HANGING CAPTAIN   P 548, $2.50

Hillary Waugh

LAST SEEN WEARING . . .   P 552, $2.40

THE MISSING MAN   P 553, $2.40

Henry Kitchell Webster

WHO IS THE NEXT?   P 539, $2.25

John Welcome

GO FOR BROKE   P 663, $2.84

RUN FOR COVER   P 664, $2.84

STOP AT NOTHING   P 665, $2.84